When Ryder's lips touched the skin at the side of Brianna's mouth, it was all she could do not to give a startled gasp as a flood of sensual feeling began to flow through her. Never had so little actual lovemaking caused such havoc!

Nothing about this encounter seemed tawdry. True, they had only met today. But when Ryder's mouth once again found hers, Brianna was lost. She grasped his back, her arms wrapping around his waist, her fingernails burying themselves in the loosened material of his shirt. She wanted him completely! At that moment, nothing seemed more important than the union of their bodies. . . .

Dear Reader,

It is our pleasure to bring you romance novels that go beyond category writing. The settings of **Harlequin American Romance** give a sense of place and culture that is uniquely American, and the characters are warm and believable. The stories are of "today" and have been chosen to give variety within the vast scope of romance fiction.

Investigative reporting is used as a vehicle to delve into the mind of a popular romance writer. Why is Brianna motivated to write romance? Is she lonely? Is she sex-starved? Ryder Cantrell actively sought this assignment to justify a personal tragedy. You decide who is the victim.

From the early days of Harlequin, our primary concern has been to bring you novels of the highest quality. **Harlequin American Romance** is no exception. Enjoy!

Vivian Stephens

Vivian Stephens
Editorial Director
Harlequin American Romance
919 Third Avenue,
New York, N.Y. 10022

Game of Hearts

GINGER CHAMBERS

Harlequin Books

TORONTO • NEW YORK • LONDON
AMSTERDAM • PARIS • SYDNEY • HAMBURG
STOCKHOLM • ATHENS • TOKYO • MILAN

For Vivian

Who found the untried clump of clay,
saw something in it,
and sparked it to life.

———————————◆————————————

Published November 1983

First printing September 1983

ISBN 0-373-16032-1

Printed in Canada

Chapter One

"I loved your book—"

"I've loved all of your books!"

"And your heroes!"

"How do you ever think of all those stories?"

"Is it very hard to write a historical? How much research do you do?"

Brianna St. Clair fielded all of the remarks and questions gracefully as she sat at the autographing table positioned at the front of the bookstore, copies of her latest bestseller spread in stacks all about her. Sometimes she still felt a little strange being the focus of so much concentrated attention, but she had been successful in her career for long enough now that most of her natural reserve had finally washed away.

"Would you sign a copy for my wife, please?" a man asked. "Make it out to Dora."

Brianna flashed a friendly smile and complied, signing her name with a flourish.

"And one for my sister? Feliz—"

Again Brianna bent to her work as the next person

handed her a copy of the thick paperback with the colorful and very suggestive cover.

For another half hour the steady stream of people continued to file by. Brianna's fingers began to cramp and her smile was becoming a little strained, but still she managed to be very gracious, and her fans went away impressed.

When at last it seemed that the worst of the deluge was over, Brianna sat back and gave a tired sigh. She flexed her right hand and the gold of the rings she wore on three fingers gleamed in the artificial light. Then for the first time in two hours she was able to look up and see the world around her. It was now mid-afternoon. And it was raining. She could see the wet drops splattering on the mall's ornamental glass roof that covered a fountain area just outside the bookstore's door.

She gave another deep sigh. She hadn't counted on rain. If it continued she was going to be soaked by the time she got back to her rental car, although she supposed she could stop in at one of the neighboring shops and purchase an umbrella. Possibly she shouldn't have dismissed the car and driver her agent had insisted be provided in each city of her tour. But she had been in either airplanes, chauffeured cars, bookstores, or hotels for the past three weeks, and she was tired of them. She had wanted to have some time away from the stifling confines and see something of this city and the next. Not that she had all that much time—at least not here. She was scheduled to be in San Antonio tomorrow. But from there she was free.

Ever since she was a little girl growing up in rural Pennsylvania she had been fascinated by things Texas. And when she had heard that Texas was to be the last state on her sweep through the southwest, a germ of an idea for a new book had come into her head, and she had insisted that San Antonio be the last of her bookings. There was something so very romantic about the old city, and, as well, it contained one of the better research facilities in the state, the Institute of Texan Cultures, which she fully intended to haunt in order to gather material.

Brianna's thoughts were brought abruptly back to the present by the prompting of another fan.

"Are you Brianna St. Clair?" a disbelieving female voice inquired.

"Yes," Brianna smiled. Her photo was plastered on a poster beside her, but this wasn't the first time she had been asked that question.

"Are you? Are you really?" the woman squeaked.

Again Brianna concurred, a smile playing lightly around her lips.

"Yes."

"Oh!" The woman let out an ear-piercing squeal. "I can't believe it! I can't believe I'm really meeting you! I've read all of your books and I love them. I just love them! The men are so sexy...and the love scenes! Do you get as turned on writing them as we do when we read them?"

Brianna cringed a little on the inside but kept her smile firmly in place.

"Sometimes," she answered honestly.

"Oh!" A curly brown head bobbed. "I knew it! I didn't see how it could be any other way. The feeling you put into them—"

Brianna interrupted the woman's gushing. It wasn't that she didn't like hearing about how well she wrote. All writers loved to be told that, but the woman was speaking so loudly that she felt as if for her own protection she had to calm her down.

"Would you like me to sign—"

She wasn't allowed to finish. "Do you live the lives of your heroines? I mean"—avid eyes roamed Brianna's face—"you look like one. In fact, you look a lot like this one." She picked up the book and studied it. "You really do! The same nose and mouth...those green eyes...the same thick blond hair. Is there a Brandon in your life? Or a Wulfgar? Or maybe both?"

"I believe you have me confused with another writer," Brianna murmured, the color in her cheeks becoming more pronounced as she noticed that a man standing nearby, one whom she had noticed earlier, was now openly listening to their conversation.

"I do?" The woman all but shouted. "Oh, yes... they are someone else's characters. Kathleen Woodiwiss, isn't it?"

Uncomfortably Brianna nodded.

Not deterred by her mistake, the woman read aloud from the teaser page just inside the front cover.

"'The shimmering heat rising from the desert sand was nothing to compare to the fire that scorched into pulsating life in Desmond's loins as he beheld Dianna's naked form.

"'In her shame Dianna could raise her violet gaze no higher than his midsection. But when she saw the evidence of his hardening manhood that the tight material of his uniform could not disguise, her eyes widened and she lifted them wonderingly to his.

"'"Desmond?" she whispered questioningly, longingly.'"

By the time the woman was done even more eyes had turned toward the table.

Brianna was embarrassed, not because of what she had written but by the insensitive way in which it had been read.

"Sounds nice and meaty to me," the woman pronounced. "Sure, yeah—sign me a copy."

After finding out her name, it was all Brianna could do not to write: "To the most boorish person I have ever met." But by remembering all the countless number of women and men who made up for the occasional clod, she signed sweetly: "Best wishes," and added her name. The woman moved away pacified.

Brianna couldn't help the relieved expulsion of breath she gave as she sat back in her chair and watched the woman's departing form. She believed there was a saying about there being one in every crowd.

Her eyes swept the store. Everyone was back to looking at what they had been before the titillating passage had been read—everyone with the exception of the man who had twice before caught her eye. He was still looking at her, and amusement was written on his expression.

Brianna's green eyes flashed over him, for the first

time examining him fully. He was well dressed, in a three-piece suit that he looked comfortable wearing. His dark brown hair was styled, the slight curling texture razor-cut to accentuate a strong-featured face on which his nose jutted prominently. He was not a handsome man, but there was something about him— Maybe it was his smile, or the way his dark eyes crinkled at the corners. Or maybe it was the air of assurance he maintained. Whatever it was, Brianna found him interesting, so when he put down the book he had been looking at and sort of ambled over to stand beside the table, she smiled up at him and asked wryly, "Are you a historical romance fan too?"

His smile deepened as he acknowledged her reference to the woman who had just left. The creases in his cheeks lengthened and a whoosh of immediate attraction shot through Brianna's body. Closer on, he was still not handsome in the accepted sense, but if physical magnetism were measured on a scale from one to one hundred, he would be right at the top.

A little breathlessly she waited for him to speak. Maybe he would have a terribly grating voice. That happened sometimes. Men, and women too, often gave one impression, and as soon as they opened their mouths, whether from the words they said or the tone of their voices, immediately disappointed their listeners.

His reply was a long time in coming. "I suppose I could do with a 'meaty' read." Clint Eastwood, Robert Redford, Paul Newman...eat your hearts out! That was the only thought that came into her brain.

His voice was like smooth, rich velvet cream with only the barest traces remaining of a Texas twang. But her Eastern ear caught it and reveled in it.

A trill of excitement fluttered in her stomach and her fingers reacted by trembling slightly. "What's your name?" she asked, and when he just continued to look at her, she hastened to add, "Unless you would rather I dedicate it to someone else."

Like a wife maybe?

"Ryder. Ryder Cantrell."

That fit. He should not be known by any other name.

Controlling the increased loss of muscle coordination in her fingers, Brianna wrote her usual little line and signed her name. For the life of her she could think of nothing special to say. And if she had, what could she scribble? "You have got the potential of being one of the most fascinating men I have ever met. And if you don't mind, could I kiss you and see if that will be as special as everything else seems to be about you?" The man would either think her mad or take her up on it—and she wasn't sure if she wanted either.

"Wild Desert Flower." He repeated the name emblazoned on her book as he picked it up to examine it more closely. Then he looked from the cover to her and back again. "She does look like you."

Much to Brianna's consternation, a light blush painted her cheeks a somewhat darker shade. "Yes. That was done on purpose. My heroine happened to have green eyes and blond hair and the artist thought it would be fun to use me as a model. They do that sometimes.''

She could see that his eyes had lowered to take in the heroine's lack of substantial clothing.

"Hmmm" was his only comment, but when he looked back at her she felt his eyes travel as far down as the table allowed.

Brianna moved uneasily. The rest of the heroine's body did bear a striking resemblance to her own— both were slender yet with larger than normal breasts for someone their slightly less than average size. But meeting the artist and posing for a snapshot, fully clothed, was as far as Brianna had gone. The rest came strictly from the man's imagination. That he had been unerringly accurate, she had put down to having a good eye.

Ryder Cantrell had the sophistication to say nothing. He read the inside teaser that the woman had read aloud and then the back that condensed the story. "Sounds pretty good—I think I'll curl up with it tonight.''

I know the story. Would you like to curl up with me? I'll tell it to you. The words almost leaped from her tongue, but she had the intelligence to stop them. God! What was happening to her?

"I hope you'll enjoy it," she said instead.

"I think I will.''

A little silence sprang up between them as Brianna began to busy herself by signing the few remaining copies of her book that were left on the table. She had already stayed on past her assigned time.

"Looks like you were pretty successful," he observed.

"Yes. This was a particularly good one."

"Aren't all your signings good?" he asked curiously.

Brianna gave a small laugh. "Now it's getting to be true, but you should have seen me a few years ago when I was first starting. I could hardly give my books away. People stayed home in droves."

"Now, that I can't imagine."

"Well, it's true." She glanced up while she closed the last book. "I didn't have the publisher behind me— I hadn't proved myself yet—or maybe it was because I didn't have an agent then. Anyway, I arranged a few signings on my own and sold a few books. Oh, the people might come back later and buy one, but most of the time they looked at me as if I were some kind of freak." She laughed. "And, believe me, there were times when I felt like one."

"But you certainly never looked like one."

Brianna shrugged. She had always taken the way she looked philosophically. Some people were physically attractive; some were not. That she happened to be was purely a genetic accident. She could have as easily been disfigured.

A woman hurried over and reached between them to hug one of Brianna's books to her bosom. "I'm so glad I got here before they were all gone. Has she already left?"

Brianna took a moment to share her gentle humor at the woman's naïve question with the man. "No, she's still here," she replied softly. "I'm Brianna St. Clair."

"Oh!" The older woman blinked, startled. "Oh—"

"Would you like me to put your name?"

"Oh, would you?" The reverence with which she answered was good for Brianna's writer's soul.

When she was done, she handed the book back to the woman who immediately replaced it at her breast. "I've read every one of your books." She listed the titles and this time they were Brianna's. "And I love them—all of them. Are you going to have another one out soon?"

"Sometime next summer."

"Good—don't stop."

"I won't," Brianna promised.

When the woman was gone, Brianna pushed away from the table. The man remained where he had been standing throughout. Brianna was aware of him with every atom of her being. He wasn't tall. If he had been she would have felt her usual pigmy as she did when standing close to a man who was over six foot. Instead, he must have been around five nine or so because with her heels the top of her head at least reached his chin. And since she was just five foot—

"Are you through here?" His warm voice called for her attention.

Brianna's green eyes shifted to look at him. Did he have a reason for asking? She hoped so.

"Yes."

"Have you had lunch?"

Her heart actually skipped a beat. She had written

of that thing happening to her heroines, but she had never experienced it before in life. In fact, she had never been sure that it could actually happen. But it did and it had and she smiled.

"No."

"Will you give me one more one-word answer?" he asked. "Would you like to have lunch with me?"

When she hesitated a moment before answering, he must have thought she was debating the issue of going out with a man she had only met a few moments before. In actuality, she was having to restrain herself from jumping up and down with uncontrolled joy. She wanted to get to know this man. And if he hadn't asked, she would have. Only it was better that he had—just for old times' sake.

"Do you have a place in mind?" she said by way of acceptance.

He smiled, his assurance not having received any jolt from her pause. "Do you?"

"I don't know Dallas. I've never been here before. So it's your choice."

He smiled again. And if it was a little self-satisfied, Brianna couldn't fault him.

"Then I'll decide. There's a place not too far away from here."

Brianna glanced up at the glass roof and was relieved to see that the sun was now shining. She wouldn't need to worry about purchasing an umbrella.

The restaurant he took her to was exactly what she would have expected from him. Quiet, understated, yet with an appeal that grew with each moment that passed. She had turned down his offer to drive her, instead following him in her rental car. She had done this in order to feel more independent. She had a special feeling for him, but she wasn't entirely stupid either.

The table they were directed to afforded a high degree of privacy, and after ordering a before-dinner drink, Brianna was able to lean back in the cushioned chair and give an appreciative, relaxing sigh. She smiled when she saw that he was observing her with a smile. She liked the way his mouth curved up on the edges in an easy, almost lazy, pull of muscle that made little creases in the sides of his cheeks.

"Tired?" he asked softly.

Brianna nodded. "Very."

"Have you been doing this long—promoting your book, I mean."

"Since the first of the month."

The waiter arrived with their drinks and Brianna took a sip of her wine while he pushed his Scotch aside. She could feel the play of his dark eyes on her face.

"Is Brianna St. Clair your real name, or do I call you something else?"

Brianna lowered her glass but kept her fingers along its cool surface. She needed the contact.

"No, Brianna is my name." Her green eyes swept up to meet his. This close she could see that they were a dark, dark blue—not the deep brown she had thought—with a thick gathering of short black lashes.

A spark of something intense seemed to quiver in the air between them.

"It's very beautiful...." His words lingered.

Brianna could find no answer as a sensation of pleasure curled its way through her body. *He's seducing me,* a small part of her brain rationalized. *With his presence, with his words, with his eyes.... I know what he's doing and I don't mind—not in the least.*

"Thank you," she whispered at last, a warmth in her own voice that he could not possibly mistake.

His smile deepened.

"Where do you live, Brianna?"

Her name on his lips was heaven. No one had ever been able to put quite that much feeling into the saying of it before.

"In Pennsylvania. A small town not far from Pittsburgh."

"You're a long way from home."

"Yes."

Magic—he was magic—this feeling was magic. She had never experienced anything like it before.

"Is there someone special waiting for you there?"

The flicker of excitement continued to build. "Just my cat—but he's been staying at my sister's and since she has three young children, he's probably not missing me." She attempted a light laugh.

He drank some of his Scotch. When he turned back to her, his eyes narrowed. "Surely there must be someone beside your cat. You're what—twenty-three, twenty-four...?"

"I'm twenty-six. And no, just Cat."

"Are all the men in Pennsylvania blind—or just stupid?"

The dry question had an edge to it. A little uneasily Brianna admitted, "Neither. There's just no one important now."

"Ah."

"What, ah?" She tried to tease.

"Well, I didn't think you could write the kind of books you do without having had a lot of...experience."

Now he was touching on a raw nerve. She had heard that line before. She countered, "Do people who write books about murderers have to go out and take a life?"

"Are you telling me that you're an innocent?"

A light flush of annoyance crept into her cheeks. "No, but—"

"I didn't think so."

At that instant Brianna wasn't sure if she liked him as much as she had thought. He was beginning to sound like one of those people who had set ideas that no amount of explanation could change. She looked down at her drink, disappointment her primary emotion.

For several moments neither of them spoke, then his hand came out to lightly touch her arm.

"Are you angry with me?" he asked softly. Brianna raised her eyes. "Because if you are, I'm sorry. I didn't mean to offend you."

A ray of hope again began to shine. At least he was man enough to apologize. She shrugged. "It's okay."

"Good. Because I wouldn't want to do anything to make you want to leave. I'm enjoying being with you too much."

The arrival of the waiter prevented her need to make a reply, and she watched as Ryder Cantrell ordered their meal after checking with her as to her likes and dislikes, and agreeing to the specialty of the house: a mouthwatering veal served with fresh vegetables and light cream sauce.

"How long have you been writing, Brianna?" he asked when again they were alone.

Brianna relaxed her guard, the magic she had felt so strongly before once again flowing.

"Since I was about ten."

"What did you write then?"

"Oh, poetry . . . and I kept a kind of journal."

"Of the people you knew, things that happened?"

"Yes."

"When did you start writing seriously?"

Brianna didn't mind his questions; to her it showed his interest. "After I sold my first manuscript—I was twenty."

"That's pretty young."

"Yes."

He smiled. "How do you find your characters? Are they people you know?"

"Sometimes," she admitted.

"Don't they object to being put in a novel? I mean, surely some of the characterizations aren't complimentary."

Brianna became serious. He really *was* interested.

Maybe he was a novice writer himself—and if there was one thing in the world she liked to do, it was to encourage new writers.

"Well, if that's the case, you never write them in such a way that they would recognize themselves. You change names, features, sometimes even sexes."

"You've done that before?"

Brianna thought of the novel she was promoting on this tour. "Yes. In *Wild Desert Flower* there's a character like the new president of the company my father works for. The man is a complete womanizer," she confided. "He's approached me—he's even approached my mother! Of course my father doesn't know about any of this. He's almost ready to retire and we don't want him to do anything that would endanger his position. So we've kept quiet. But this is my revenge. I've made him the owner of a tavern where my heroine is a servant, and he's the scum of the earth. There couldn't possibly be anyone more slimy or repulsive."

"That sounds like a good story in itself," he murmured.

"It is."

"And you've done this before?"

"A few times, but not always with people I've got something against. I have a good friend who's the model for one of my heroines. But most of my characters are fictional."

A lazy smile again pulled at his lips. "What about me? Will I ever be in one of your books?"

Brianna pretended to look him over carefully. In

reality she didn't need to. She had memorized every plane and valley of his strongly put-together face, every dark hair that crisply curled its way to his neck. "Oh, you'd definitely be hero material," she decided at last.

"I've always thought the villain was much more interesting," he murmured.

Brianna grinned. "Me too. There's something about all that evilness and vileness."

"Oh, definitely."

"All right," she decided. "You'll be a villain."

He laughed. "I expect to receive a copy."

"I'll even dedicate it to you."

His dark blue eyes were warm and Brianna experienced a thrill at how close a rapport they had going so quickly. She knew nothing about him; she had been too busy answering his questions to ask any of her own, but there were some things mere words could not convey.

The delivery of their meal brought her back to reality, or at least a portion of it. She couldn't say if the veal was prepared well or if the sauce was perfection. All she did was mechanically eat and make an occasional reply to his appreciative statements.

While they waited for dessert, another specialty of the house—fresh strawberries smothered in cream— he mused, "You're very quiet."

"I was just enjoying the silence."

"Have I asked too many quesions?"

Brianna sat forward. 'Oh, no! I didn't mean that. It's just that I'm glad this tour is almost over."

"Is Dallas the last city on your itinerary?"

"No. San Antonio."

He was silent for a moment before saying, "I live in San Antonio."

Brianna's heart speeded up. "You do?"

"Uh-huh." His hand came out to cover hers.

Her pulse began to race. She tried to retain a surface calm. "Are you here on business?"

"You could say that."

"Are you married?" There—get the all-important question over and done with. The last man she had gone out with had neglected to impart the fact of his marriage until their third and last date.

"No. I was, but it didn't work out."

A twinge of jealousy for the unknown woman who had once had claim on him shot through Brianna. Then telling herself she was being ridiculous, she asked, "How long are you going to be in Dallas?"

"Another couple of days."

"I leave tomorrow."

"Morning or evening?"

"Morning."

For a few moments he said nothing, and as the silence lengthened, Brianna's nerves tightened.

"What are you doing this afternoon?" he asked at last.

"I have another signing scheduled."

"What time?"

"Two o'clock."

"Where?"

"At a bookstore across town."

"Let me take you there."

"But my car—"

"We'll drop it off at your hotel. Where are you staying?"

"The Sheraton."

Ryder looked deeply into her eyes, and she read a wealth of promise in his gaze. "All right," she whispered softly. She knew she might be agreeing to more than he was asking right at this moment, but she truly didn't care. She would deal with that problem later. Right now she didn't want to be separated from him. She liked being near him, liked the way he made her feel.

They left their dessert only partially eaten, and as they made their way from the restaurant, Ryder placed his hand at the base of her back. She felt the touch through the material of her dress and for all the emotional tumult it caused within her, he could have been caressing her bare skin.

All the way to her hotel Brianna was aware of the sleek black Corvette following her. And several times while she waited for traffic lights to change she was drawn to look into her rearview mirror. Each time he saw her glance, he smiled that slow easy smile that made her heart do its flip.

Could this really be happening? she asked herself. Was it for real? Normally she was not the type of woman to pick up a man—and that was exactly the term for what she had done. What did she know about him except that she was strongly attracted to him? But did she have to know more? Couldn't she just accept that fact without introspection as she had been doing since she had first met him? Couldn't she just let nature take its course? Other women did. Why should she be different? Couldn't she, for once in her life, be just like everyone else—take what came and not worry about tomorrow?

Brianna's face held a calm resolve when she emerged from her car in the parking garage. Damn it all, she *would* be like other women. She was not going to let outdated morals stand in her way. She wrote of women who flew in the face of convention; now she was going to be one!

Ryder pushed the car door open from inside and waited for her to take her place in the bucket seat next to his.

"Are you ready?" he asked, his eyes following her movement as she adjusted her skirt over her slender thighs.

That inquiry seemed appropriate. "For anything!" she returned, turning to him.

He only smiled.

She hadn't expected him to wait while she spent her required time at the bookstore. Yet he did. He stayed close beside her, seemingly interested in each and every person who came to request her autograph.

Finally when the two hours had passed, the store's manager came to thank her for coming.

"When will your next book be out?" she was pressed. "Did I hear you say something about next June?"

"That's when it's scheduled to be released," Brianna answered. "I've just turned in the final draft."

"Good. These people are such fans of yours. They keep asking and asking. Now I'll have something to tell them."

The woman's speculative gaze went from Brianna to Ryder, but Brianna didn't feel like making introductions any more now than when they had first arrived. Just how Ryder fit into her life was no one's business but her own. And she didn't like the way the manager's eyes took on a gleam of physical appreciation whenever they alighted on him.

So instead she expressed her appreciation for all the work the manager had done to ensure the success of the autographing, and then she nodded to Ryder, who took her arm and accompanied her out the door.

Once they were inside his car, Brianna leaned back against the tall headrest and closed her eyes, feeling drained. It took a lot out of a person to be charming, especially when one didn't feel that way. Sitting in a chair signing books had been the last thing she had wanted to be doing, squandering the precious moments she had in Dallas... with Ryder.

"How many more of these do you have to do?" Ryder's question broke into her thoughts.

"Here? None. This was the last. In San Antonio I have two."

"You look exhausted. When you finish, are you going to take some time off and get some rest, or are you going to go home and plunge into another story?"

Brianna turned her head, her partially closed eyes

taking in the fact that he had removed the jacket to his suit before sliding in behind the wheel. Now she could see that his vest and shirt hugged a trim, taut waist and shoulders that looked powerful even under the confines of material.

"I plan on staying in San Antonio for a while."

He spared a quick glance away from the road. His dark eyes were bright with a strange kind of irony. They were teasing, yet they were smug. Did he think she was saying that only because he had told her he lived there? Quickly she decided to rectify his conclusion.

"I'm going to do some research."

Again a strange smile tilted his lips. Just what kind of research did he think she meant? Had he jumped to the unwarranted conclusion that she still was involving him? Was he just like so many other men who had decided she was fair game because she dealt with sex in her books in an open and honest way? Was that why there were times when, even though she was tremendously attracted to him—had decided that she had never met another man quite like him and very much wanted to learn more—she didn't like him very much?

"Do you have another idea for a book?" he asked interestedly and so smoothly that she began to doubt her earlier misgivings.

Brianna frowned slightly, then pushed her indecision away. She was not going to look too deeply at anything. What happened, would happen. Hadn't she already decided that?

"Yes."

"What is it?"

Brianna sighed and shifted her position in the seat. "I'm not sure yet."

Ryder laughed. "You don't want to tell me?"

"No, it's not that." She tucked a long strand of honey-blond hair back behind one ear. How could she explain? Especially when she didn't completely understand her creative processes herself. "It's just that I *can't* tell you. I feel something, but I haven't settled on it yet. And I want to take some time to study."

"Study?"

"Yes."

"What would you have to study?"

Again Brianna felt the tug of irritation. She had thought more of him. "Everything! I write historicals, remember? And they don't write themselves. I have to decide on a period, then do all kinds of research—what people wore, what they used in their everyday lives, how they talked, how they thought about things, what was happening in the world around them. Like I said, everything!"

"Then you write the book."

"Then I write the book."

"How long does it take you?"

"From the time I first start?"

He nodded.

"About a year, sometimes more."

He glanced at her again. "Isn't that a little slow? I mean, I've heard of some writers taking only a few weeks."

Brianna's temper sizzled. "Do you want to continue on a friendly basis?" she demanded.

Ryder seemed a little startled by her sudden vehemence. "Yes."

"Then don't compare me to other people. I'm me. It takes me at least a year and sometimes longer when my research runs over."

He was amused. "Okay. I won't say anything more. And I definitely won't compare you to anyone else." He paused and again those dark blue eyes met hers. "Anyway, I can't imagine there being another person like you anywhere in the world."

"Thank you," she said abruptly, accepting his compliment. "There isn't."

Now his humor increased. "Is ego ever a problem for you?"

That question brought Brianna's impatience back into perspective. He hadn't really meant anything derogatory by what he had said. He didn't know how she prided herself on the accuracy of her research and how much effort it took to weave the information skillfully into her plots.

"By the sound of that last reply, it would seem so... but not really." She lifted one shoulder slightly. "It's just that I get asked that question a lot. And some people never understand that writing is work. They think it's some sort of sham—even to the point of believing that there is an entire bank of computers sitting in some large room that turn out the books they read."

"Untouched by human hands," he murmured.

"Right," she agreed.

One of his hands fell from the steering wheel to cover one of hers. Slowly he turned it over and began to circle a finger along her palm.

"This hand looks very sensitive."

Brianna's breathing quickened. Whenever he touched her everything seemed to short circuit inside her. As if, in a storm, electrical charges were going off like exploding fireworks.

When she made no reply, he returned his hand to the steering wheel. Some seconds later he asked, "Are you in a hurry to get back to your hotel?"

Brianna still had not recovered from his touch. "No," she answered, her throat tight.

"Then why don't we take a little drive. I know a place where you can really relax."

"Sounds good to me," she agreed, her blood retaining its unsettled life.

Again he smiled.

Chapter Two

The drive did not last long—or at least it didn't seem long to Brianna. She was content to let the miles fly by, enjoying the quiet hum of the car's engine and the soft music that was playing on the stereo system. In fact she drifted in and out of a light sleep, one moment overwhelmingly aware of where she was, and the next floating on some sylvan cloud, dreaming of the silent man beside her. When they approached their destination, it took a touch from Ryder Cantrell to bring her fully back to awareness.

"Wake up, Sleeping Beauty. We're here." His words were soft and huskily spoken.

Brianna slowly opened her eyes, the unusual green color closely repeated in the dress she wore. She was looking directly into his face. He was resting one arm along the steering wheel and leaning toward her, the other arm crooked at the elbow so that his hand could grasp the headrest of her seat. Out of necessity, in the small confines of the car, he was very close.

Brianna blinked once in surprise, a section of her

mind grappling with the fact that the car had stopped, but the majority of her thoughts centered on the man who was only a short move away.

"Where are we?" she asked, her question barely above a whisper.

For a long breathless moment he only looked at her. Then he countered, "Does it matter?"

"No," she admitted softly.

"Then don't worry about it. We're at an old inn— that's all you need to know."

A faint dreamy tilt of lips showed her approval.

Again Ryder's gaze went slowly over her face, sliding with lingering ease from feature to feature—from wide-spaced eyes above delicately formed cheekbones to perfect nose and on to her extremely kissable mouth. A rush of feeling darkened his eyes to an even more intense blue, and gradually he leaned closer.

Brianna remained perfectly still. She had been waiting for this moment from almost the first instant she saw him. When his lips met hers, it was everything she had wondered it would be. She had been kissed many times in her life—more than kissed. But she had never before known such a surge of clamoring, sensual pleasure. It was almost as if they had blended together instantly; as if, with the mingling of that small section of their bodies, they were united by emotional bonds that transcended mere physical contact.

Without deepening the kiss any further—could he possibly have felt the same sense of wonder as she?—Ryder pulled away. There was no trace of his earlier lighthearted approach. He was gazing back at her seriously, his breath matching hers in the increased rise and fall of his chest. Then his expression lightened, and he gave a self-mocking smile.

"I believe I told you I was bringing you here to relax."

Brianna appreciated his wry way of looking at the situation. "And if I told you I was relaxed?"

The creases on either side of his mouth deepened. "I wouldn't believe you."

Without giving a second thought, Brianna reached up to touch the thick dark hair that grew from his temple back above his ear.

"You would be right."

He caught her hand and brought it to his lips.

"Is this the way your heroes do it in your books?" He proceeded to kiss the inside of her wrist, his tongue gently caressing the tender skin.

Brianna wanted to melt in the seat. First one assault on her senses, then another...and she wasn't sure which was the more shattering.

"Yes," she breathed. Then in an attempt to keep a small measure of equilibrium she reminded him, "But you told me you wanted to be the villain."

His lazy smile appeared, and he looked at her over her own wrist. "I am; I do—but villains aren't always just the antiheroes. Don't they ever have any redeeming qualities? For instance, don't they sometimes love and want the heroine, sincerely want her, only something, some flaw, keeps them away?"

Brianna looked at him with a surprised expression in her eyes. "Yes, you're right. But I didn't expect—"

"There are all kinds of heroes, Brianna. And all

kinds of villains. Sometimes it's hard to tell them apart."

Brianna made no reply. What he was saying was true.

"Now, if I remember correctly what I read about this place," he said, shifting subjects, "they should be serving dinner. Are you hungry?"

Brianna watched as he released the catch on his door and uncoiled his length from the seat. She couldn't believe he was hungry again. She certainly wasn't. At least not for food. But if she didn't want to be left sitting in the car, she decided she had better follow his example.

"Not really," she replied when they were walking side by side toward the two-story wood-frame building. "Are you?"

"Sure. I'm starving. I'm still a growing boy. My daddy always said that a man didn't stop growing until his hair turned completely white, and sometimes, with luck, not even then. Now, I'm not sure if he meant physically or intellectually. But right now I'll settle for physically."

Brianna laughed in spite of herself. "And just how old are you?"

"Running close to forty. Thirty-eight, actually. Is that too old?"

He had a habit of disconcerting her with questions— some she could answer easily and others she could not. She tried with this one.

"Too old for what?"

"Chasing young girls like you."

Her laughter bubbled over. She was finding that trying to keep up with him was like trying to capture quicksilver. One minute he was one person, the next another. She decided to play along.

"I suppose it depends on what you plan to do with me when you catch me."

His grin became lecherous as he guided her through the gate of a white picket fence. "Why evil, naturally."

"Then I'll be sure to hurry a little slower...just to be sure."

He paused at the door and pretended to look up toward the sky in thought. "I wonder if there's a feminine equivalent to a dirty old man?"

"Why?" she questioned. "Do you want to find one?"

He grinned down at her. "I think I already have."

Then he opened the door and gave her a gentle nudge to go in before him.

As she had told Ryder before they entered the inn, she was not really very hungry, the meal they had shared at lunch having filled her. But as soon as her nose detected the delicious aromas coming from the direction of the kitchen, she immediately found that there was just possibly a little spare room in her stomach, and she acquiesced when he told her that this restaurant was famous for its Texas-style chicken fried steak, a delicious rendering of tenderized steak, breaded and deep fried until golden brown.

The atmosphere of the old inn was fascinating to Brianna. Being a writer of historial fiction, she was naturally a lover of history, and the room they were in could easily have been at home in the past century:

high-ceilinged with fans gently moving the air, old-fashioned wallpaper, long windows open to let the lace curtains stir, various keepsakes lovingly preserved. It was as if they had taken a step back in time.

"You like it?" Ryder prompted.

Brianna's eyes were shining. "I like it."

"They have guest rooms too."

"Oh?" She was very much aware of him.

"I've heard that they're something to see as well, that is if you like this sort of thing."

Brianna's heart was beginning to pound. She wasn't exactly sure what she should say next. One of her heroines would know—but then, if what the character said was wrong, all she had to do was rewrite. In real life it wasn't that simple.

The necessity for a reply was taken from her hands though when Ryder leaned back in his chair and continued, "But I also understand that the better rooms go quickly and that you have to put in your reservation several weeks in advance."

"Yes, I would imagine so." Brianna's outward reaction was calm and cool, but inside she was a mass of contradictory feelings: Excitement vied mightily with disappointment; relief with annoyance. Had she mistaken his meaning?

"Then again too, the smaller rooms are probably just as nice," he went on to say, causing Brianna to feel as if she were on a carnival ride—one minute up, the next down.

Just what was he trying to say? She decided to take a measure of control.

"Yes, they probably are. I wonder if the manager would mind giving us a tour?"

Ryder's eyes crinkled at the corners, and his lips turned up into a slow smile.

"I don't know. Do you want one?"

Brianna was in no state of mind to say exactly what she did want. All she knew was that she was beginning to feel extremely frustrated. If he wanted her to stay the night with him, why didn't he just come right out and ask? So far he had not struck her as being shy. But maybe being that blunt wasn't a part of his style. And *she* wasn't about to suggest it!

"No, not really. At least not now."

"You still look very tired."

As in "you look like a hag"? Maybe she better go check; she had made no repairs to her appearance since before the first signing this morning.

"I am." She looked around but could see no discreetly marked sign.

A frown was settling on her brow when Ryder said, "Come on. I know where they are. I saw them earlier."

Brianna's cheeks were tinged with pink when she stood up. Had she been that obvious?

Five minutes later they were both reseated at their small table and a huge platter of breaded steak, mashed potatoes, and green beans was resting before each of them.

Brianna's eyes took in the size of the portion. "I don't think I'm going to be able to eat even half of this!" she cried in dismay.

"Sure you are."

"I don't think so," Brianna countered doubtfully, shaking her head.

But she did. She was embarrassed by the amount of food she did eventually eat. Not everything, it was true. But a great deal more than half. The only blessing she could count was that Ryder had completely finished his and, as well, the large slice of thick buttered toast that accompanied it.

Brianna gave a soft moan as they walked back to the car. "I don't think I want to see food again for a week!"

Ryder glanced at her and tightened the arm he had placed around her shoulders. "To tell you the truth, neither do I."

"We'll have to go on a diet!" Brianna said, then began to giggle. "But it was so *good*!"

"Well worth all the pain we'll have to suffer," Ryder agreed teasingly.

The sound of their laughter echoed in the swiftly falling dusk.

The total darkness of night had completely enclosed the city when they again arrived at her hotel. Only man-made lighting illuminated the nearby streets and buildings in imitation of the sun.

As Ryder drove directly into the garage, Brianna said nothing. A fine tension had begun to build in her with each spin of the car's wheels since leaving the inn and now her nerves were as taut as a cellist's bowstring.

This entire day had been something out of the ordinary. She was on her own in a city far away from her home; she was in the company of a man she had met only hours earlier. Her sister would say that she had gone temporarily insane. She would say that Ryder could be anyone: a "crazy" bent on doing ill, a person who was out for only his own self-interests and who wouldn't care what happened to her after he was gone. And she might be right. But Brianna didn't think so. Yet she was becoming uneasy. It was so simple to tell yourself that you will accept what comes when it wasn't so near to coming. What if he was a pervert? Would she be able to find help?

She jumped slightly when he opened the car door for her. She had been so deep in thought that she hadn't realized he had got out.

With her eyes wide, she looked up at him. He didn't smile back. His expression was one she had never seen before. There was absolutely no trace of humor or of feeling. He could have been a cold-blooded killer about to perform a service.

Yet, as she continued to stare, a warmth crept into his eyes, and she was partially reassured. But she couldn't quite put his previous look out of her mind.

"I am invited up for a nightcap?" he prompted.

Brianna thrust her troubling thoughts aside. She had always had a good imagination—or rather exaggerated imagination. That was why writing was such a good profession for her.

"Of course."

As she slid her legs from the car, the slit in the

side of her dress allowed a great deal of shapely thigh to show. She felt Ryder's eyes but did not meet them.

The ride up the elevator was a silent one. For the life of her Brianna could think of nothing to say that would break her tension and not sound absolutely childish.

That was why she was so amazed by herself when it came time to open the door to her suite. Her hand didn't shake; the key fit into the lock at first try. You would think she had entertained hundreds of men in her room in the past!

She latched on to this sudden surface calm and called easily, "What would you like? I'll have room service bring it up," as she put her purse on the ledge above a mock fireplace. A large mirror was fastened to the wall above and as she looked into it, she could see in between the reflected flower petals of an arranged bouquet that Ryder once again had that hard look. Yet when she turned around, it was gone.

"Bourbon," he replied, then began to look around the beautifully decorated sitting room. Coral, ice-green, some shades of blue, all combined with predominant white to make the room vibrate with life. "This is very nice," he said appreciatively.

"Only the very best!" she agreed, then wished she had never said it. It sounded so...so...crass.

To get over that uncomfortable moment, she crossed to the table where the telephone was located and made his request for liquor. For herself, she ordered coffee. Whatever was going to happen—*if* anything was going to happen—she wanted to be completely aware of it.

She turned to catch a funny smile curving Ryder's lips.

"I almost always drink coffee," she defended, all the while hating herself for feeling that she needed to do so.

His humor increased. "That's okay with me."

A minor furrow in the skin of her forehead was the only sign she gave that she was beginning to wonder if he was secretly laughing at her.

"Why don't we sit down," she suggested.

She fit action to her words, and he came to sit close beside her on the narrow sofa.

Brianna searched for something else to say. She didn't know if it was herself, or him, or what, but something wasn't right. And she didn't know what to do about it.

"Ah, have you lived in San Antonio long?" Maybe if she questioned him they would get back to the easy footing they had achieved earlier.

"All my life."

"Do you live there by choice?"

"Yes. If you have to live in a big city, San Antonio is the best place to be in Texas."

Brianna laughed uneasily. It wasn't working! "The people who live in Dallas and Houston might not agree."

He shrugged. "Then that's their hard luck."

Brianna tried another track.

"What do you do? I mean, what do you do for a living?"

Instantly she felt his deep blue eyes fasten onto her, and—she could hardly believe it—there was an immediate stiffening of his body. But closely following was an enforced relaxation, so that when he answered, it was a droll, ''I dabble in real estate.''

A quiet knock on her door signaled the arrival of their order. Quickly Brianna jumped to her feet and hurried to answer it. She wondered what Ryder would do if she begged the waiter to join them. But she did no such thing. She signed the receipt and resumed her seat on the sofa, where before them rested an array of choices: a bucket of ice, a full bottle of liquor, glasses, a carafe, two cups and saucers, two spoons, small containers of sugar and cream. The kitchen had thought of everything.

''Would you like some coffee? There seems to be more than enough.''

Ryder leaned forward and flipped a glass over. ''No, thanks.'' He ignored the ice and poured a measure of the dark amber liquid. When he was done, he started to recap the bottle, but stopped and asked, ''Do you want some of this?''

Then suddenly something about the situation seemed to strike him as funny. And this time Brianna didn't mind. This wasn't the same kind of brittle humor he had exhibited a few moments before. It was much more like the give and take they had enjoyed during their sojourn at the inn.

''No thanks,'' she returned in kind, smiling. She reached for the carafe.

Ryder sat back, easing his long legs and letting his

left arm rest along the back of the sofa. He swallowed a portion of his drink.

"Where are you staying when you get to San Antonio? Another place like this?" He motioned to the richness of their surroundings.

"For a few days, yes. Then I'm going to find somewhere else. I'm tired of living in hotels." Brianna stirred sugar in her coffee before she too leaned back.

"Yeah. I know what you mean. This kind of living is nice. But after a while you get to where you'd give everything you own for the right to throw a TV dinner into your oven and eat it in the confines of your favorite chair."

Brianna began to laugh. That so aptly described the way she felt, although she would never have used just that phraseology. She had never liked to live out of suitcases, and one of the first things she had decided about remaining in San Antonio for a month or so was that she would definitely find some place other than a hotel to stay—preferably a small house, or an apartment.

"You're right," she agreed, then sobered. "Did you say you have something to do with real estate? Do you know of any place—"

"I don't deal in houses," he interrupted abruptly.

"Oh."

His easy smile appeared again. "But I know some people who do. Tell me where you're staying and I'll send someone your way."

"At the Marriott."

"By the Paseo del Rio."

"What's that?"

"You'll find out."

She smiled. "Are you so sure?"

"Definitely. You won't be able to miss it."

"I won't need a guide?"

"No, if you lean too far over your hotel balcony, you'll fall in."

"Sounds interesting."

"Mmmm."

For the last second or two, Ryder's eyes had been growing warmer as they more closely examined the intricacies of her features. Then the hand that had been spread along the cushioned sofa back moved until his fingers could touch the smooth soft texture of her long golden hair.

Brianna shivered at the gentle stroking action.

"You have beautiful hair. It's like spun honey." He leaned his face near enough to bury his nose in the thickness. "And it smells good too...fresh...."

Brianna closed her eyes. This seemed to be the beginning of the moment she had been preparing for—a continuation of what had started in the car outside the inn.

With one easy move Ryder straightened and put his drink down on the table, then he relieved her of her untouched coffee, placing the cup on the table as well. After that, he began a slow caressing of the side of her cheek.

"So soft and smooth," he breathed huskily.

Brianna's breath caught in her throat.

When his lips touched the skin at the side of her mouth, it was all she could do not to give a startled gasp as a flood of sensual feeling began to flow through her. Never had so little actual lovemaking caused such havoc! What would more do?

She soon found out. Instead of moving to cover her mouth, his lips glided instead to her ear, there to lightly follow the small outline, grazing the skin with the tip of his tongue, before trailing along her jawline to her chin, where at last they came to a stop. But the pause was designed only as a tantalizing prompting for her to open her eyes.

Almost unwillingly they fluttered open. And when they did, Brianna saw the glitter of arousal lying freshly banked in his deep blue gaze, saw the determination, saw...something else. But she couldn't decipher what it was and soon let it drift away. She was too caught up in what she was feeling to wonder for long.

Her full mouth parted slightly, and it was as if that was the signal Ryder had been waiting for. Without delay his mouth covered hers, moving, devouring, causing electrical impulses of growing desire to instantly shoot from one sensitive nerve ending to the next.

Her arms came up to encircle his neck, pulling him to her, showing him her enjoyment of what was being done, encouraging him to do more. Her fingers threaded in the crisp texture of his hair.

With no hesitation, Ryder responded, further deepening the kiss, his arm around her waist crushing her to him, his hand at the back of her head increasing its pressure.

Brianna became a creature of sensation. She liked the clean taste of him, the hard, yet warm, feel of him. Liked the way he smelled—a blending of a spicy men's cologne and his own animal scent.

Not once did she try to draw back; not once did she let the little voice in the back of her consciousness speak above a distant whisper. And when his hand lowered to cover her breast, she reacted by arching her back and giving a long, low moan.

The zip to her dress was easy to undo. And almost before she was aware of it, it was released and Ryder was pulling at the straps of her bra to lower them.

When the bountiful softness was set free, Ryder himself echoed her primal moan. It came low and husky, almost as if against his will.

Through half-closed eyes Brianna leaned back against the sofa arm and watched as he bent his head to kiss each throbbing mound in turn, his tongue teasing the nipples until they were taut and hard.

When he became aware that she was watching, he met her glazed vision, the stoked fires that had earlier been coming to life in his eyes now molten.

Brianna raised a trembling finger to touch his lips; Ryder kissed it.

Then her hand lowered until she could free the buttons of his vest and, as well, the buttons of his shirt. Beneath, she found the intimate treasure she had been searching for—a fine sprinkling of dark body hair that grew on his chest and followed his flat stomach, in the loose configuration of a vee, until it disappeared beneath the belt of his pants. Her fingers tingled at the contact.

Ryder pushed her hand away and raised himself until he was lying atop her, his naked chest pressed against her breasts, his thighs pushing hers into a more satisfying arrangement. His arms carried some of his weight so that he did not completely crush her.

When his mouth once again found hers, Brianna was lost. She grasped his back, her arms wrapping around his waist, her fingernails burying themselves in the loosened material of his shirt. She never wanted to be separated from him! She wanted him completely! Nothing seemed more important than the union of their bodies.

Nothing about this encounter seemed tawdry. True, they had only met today. True, in all likelihood she would have condemned her actions in another. But then she would not have understood. It was easy to judge other people when you have never been in their position before. Easy to play God. All she knew was that this was right. Being with Ryder was right. What they were going to do was right. Maybe she had fallen instantly in love with him. Maybe all she felt was a strong attraction. But did it matter? Did she really have to feel anything but what she did?

Again the little voice tried to make itself heard—the voice of reason, of caution—but Brianna didn't hear it. This time she didn't even hear the beginnings of its last gasping cry as she rushed down the road to meet her fate.

At first Brianna didn't understand what was happening. She felt Ryder pull away; waited long seconds for his return. But when, after what seemed an aching passage of time, she opened her eyes, it was to find him standing at the opposite end of the couch, tucking his rebuttoned shirt back into the waistband of his pants.

The depth of her confusion was evident in her eyes.

"Ryder?" she questioned thickly.

His gaze swept over her, something about it making her pull the material of her dress up to cover her breasts and adjust the position of her legs and skirt.

"What is it, Ryder? What's wrong?"

His eyes never moved away as he fastened the buttons of his vest.

Brianna struggled to sit up. Her face was pale. She had never been in a position such as this before. Always it was she, the woman, who pulled away, who set the limits. Never had she known a man to change his mind. But why did it have to happen now? Just when, for the first time, she was in complete agreement about going on?

As he continued to be silent, her face became flushed with shameful color that seemed to spread throughout her body. He was making her feel as if she were some sort of scarlet woman! But why? Why had he stopped? She knew he had wanted her, had felt the hardness of his desire, had tasted his passion....

"Ryder?" she questioned again, her voice small.

Ryder looked away. It was to locate the jacket of his suit that he had earlier thrown across the back of the matching chair. He moved over to pluck it from its resting place, then folded it over one arm.

Finally he spoke. "I thought I could do it, but I can't. I have to live with myself tomorrow."

Tears welled up in Brianna's eyes, but she valiantly kept them at bay. What was he talking about?

"I've found out all I needed to know." He paused. "I warned you I was the villain."

Then on saying those totally uncomprehensible sentences, he looked at her for another moment before turning his back and letting himself quietly out the door.

How long Brianna remained immobile on the narrow sofa with his words ringing in her ears, she was never to know. But when at last she did move, she felt as if she had been turned to stone, and her joints protested with jerky movements.

It was then that a fine trembling set it, and she didn't know whether to laugh or to cry, or do both. She was so embarrassed, felt so ashamed! She had completely let the stops go on all her emotions only to have them thrown back in her face as if wanting. That had never happened to her before. The tables had been well and truly turned. But did it have to happen now? With Ryder?

Slowly, a healthy, defensive anger began to build. Just who did he think he was? Just who the holy hell did he think he was? He couldn't do that to her! She wouldn't let him!

Without further thought Brianna jumped to her

feet and ran toward the door, replacing her arms in the sleeves of her dress as she went. She could do nothing about the gaping of the zipper. There wasn't time—and anyway, it didn't matter.

She jerked the door open and leaned out to yell: "You can't do this to me, Ryder Cantrell!"

Her action just caused her more embarrassment. The elevator doors at the end of the hall were already closed and only the husband and wife who were walking along the corridor to their room next door heard her words.

Quickly Brianna stepped back into her room, the closed door safely protecting her from further mortification. Never in her entire life was she going to be able to forget the look in those people's eyes. They had seen her as some kind of tramp!

The loosely hung shoulder of her dress slipped and she automatically reached up to catch it. Then with slow steps she moved to the mirror above the fireplace. What she saw reflected there gave her little room for blaming them—her hair was rumpled, flying out away from her head in tousled disarray; her makeup was splotched; her lips devoid of artificial color and kissed into a swollen pout; her dress was half falling off. No, blame was not to be attached to them.

There was another source much more guilty. And even though she would dearly love to place the responsibility squarely on Ryder Cantrell's strong shoulders—for after all what had she done to make him react the way he had? She had only behaved as millions of men had been doing throughout the centuries and the way today's woman had attained the freedom to act. There was only one person who had made a fool of herself. And that was herself. She was adult enough to see it, to admit it, but it didn't make it hurt any less, or make her like it.

She had let herself become carried away, and with a man she knew nothing about. It was just as she had feared before they came to her room. In some ways, she supposed she was lucky. She could have suffered much, much more.

Only, what exactly had he meant when he said he had learned what he needed to know? And why did he say he had to live with himself tomorrow?

Was he only being strange? Did he go around doing this to all the women he met who let him near? Was it his idea of some kind of kinky revenge against womankind? Or was he being straight? Did his words have some meaning that she could not as yet understand? And would she ever understand?

With a rush of feeling Brianna remembered the way it was to have him make love to her, remembered the smooth texture of his skin as it pressed against her own, remembered his kisses, his touch.

Damn it all! What did she do now? Try to forget? A short, hollow laugh escaped her lips. She doubted if she would ever be able to forget. Happenings like this didn't occur every day in her life. If they did, she would think nothing of them, not be so upset.

But one thing she knew: She never wanted to see Ryder Cantrell again. Never in her life. If it were possible, she would start this day over again and totally cut him out of her existence. If she was working and he was purely a figment of her imagination, a personality creation she was debating for use in a book, she would tear his character sketch up into little pieces and flush them down the nearest commode. She would—

A grain of humor surfaced to help save Brianna's wounded pride. She supposed she would survive if she could see a little of the funny side of the situation so quickly.

Yet all the same it hurt. Her judgment was shaken, her belief in herself. And she wondered if she should keep on with her plans to stay in San Antonio. She had to go there, there was no backing out of that now. She had commitments. But when the signings were done, what should she do then?

More of Brianna's fighting spirit returned, and she gave her head a determined toss. Damn it all, she would stay. She had an idea for another book, and she wasn't going to let herself be derailed from that track. She was a professional; she had a job to do.

And anyway, what made her think she might see Ryder there? *If* he lived in San Antonio, which was a pretty big *if*, the city wasn't exactly a tiny little town. Just as in Pittsburgh, people probably came and went, lived and died, all in the same neighborhood, and didn't necessarily know each other.

All she could hope was that he wouldn't try to contact her again—which she doubted. He hadn't sounded exactly overwhelmed with her when he left.

She had an evening radio talk-show interview to-morrow and a morning television appearance the next day for publicity, but after her signings she could disappear. And only she would know that she was carrying a slightly dented shield of pride, and the determination that in her next book she would figure out a way to end the villain's life in some horribly grotesque manner. But she wouldn't dare use anyone she knew for that character—she couldn't allow his presence in her mind for as long as it would take to write about him. But she would know. And in a childish, vindictive way she would enjoy doing away with him.

A lingering smile played about Brianna's lips as she stripped off her dress and made her way to the shower where she could wash away the collected dust and humiliation of her second day in Texas.

Chapter Three

The five-hour trip from Dallas to San Antonio south-west through the central portion of the state was exhilarating as well as exhausting to Brianna. This was the first time she had driven so far completely on her own with no one to share the driving chore, and the contrasting types of scenery she passed made her long to be able to pull off of the interstate highway and investigate. She would have liked nothing better than to stop at some of the cattle ranches outside of Waco, spend the day in the state capital, Austin, and relax in the lush green river country of San Marcos and New Braunfels. But at the moment, she just didn't have the time. She had to be at the radio station for a quarter to seven, so that meant she had to already be checked into her hotel, showered, dressed, to have redone her makeup, eaten, and last of all located the station. Which put her on a tight schedule, especially when it had been nearly noon before she checked out of the hotel in Dallas.

Not that she had planned on being that late in leaving the city; it was just that after the restless night she had spent, her deepest sleep had come only toward dawn, and she had not awakened until much later than she wanted. And then her first waking thought had been of her experience the night before, which was not a good way to start her new day.

But as time passed, and her mind was able to purge itself of what had happened, her temperament improved and she thoroughly enjoyed being on her own. Air travel was wonderful in order to move from one distant place to another in a short amount of time, yet she would trade nothing for all that she had seen this day. And she was beginning to pick up a flavor, a feel for the people of this state. At the little café where she stopped for lunch, she had met an interesting woman who prided herself on the fact that her ancestors had come to Texas with Stephen F. Austin, the first non-Mexican allowed to bring settlers into the new land, which Mexico claimed at the time.

Brianna knew a little of the rich history of Texas; she knew a little of the history of many places—and a lot about the areas where her previous books had taken place. To her, what made writing so exciting was the research. She almost became obsessed each time she became involved with an era and a place, not to mention the people and how they lived. She could hardly wait for the necessary evils of these last appearances to be done with so that she could attack the institute. She wanted her book to center on the period just before Texas won its independence as a republic and concentrate on the Mexican people's reactions to the invasion of Anglos who were coming to live close by. She could see that a good love story could be found in there somewhere.

Once she arrived in San Antonio, Brianna went immediately to her hotel, where she definitely didn't take time to look out over the balcony, although she had noticed a brochure on her dresser that hyped the Paseo del Rio as being one of the greatest experiences of the area: the River Walk that hugged a portion of the San Antonio River as it meandered through the central section of the city. Brianna made a face at the brochure before turning her back on it. She knew it was silly to be prejudiced in this way toward something that was in all likelihood very beautiful, but she doubted if she would ever take the walking tour. She didn't enjoy wallowing in negative thoughts. And as proof, she didn't let the name and face of Ryder Cantrell be more than just a quick spark in the far recesses of her brain.

The radio station was much like all the others she had been in over the past few weeks. Located in a somewhat seedy section of town, it was a maze of hallways and doors that only those educated in the layout of the building could follow. She was shown into a small room where the interviewer was already seated at a desk. Through a section of glass wall she could see the control room and the men who worked there. She took her place at the desk where a microphone was aimed directly at her. Its end was covered with a spongy material that made it resemble a dark, pregnant tennis ball.

The man who was to interview her looked up and

smiled. He was middle-aged, with thinning blond hair, a slight weight problem, and his small eyes looked intelligently inquisitive. A headset was resting about his neck and he had been in the process of jotting a note on the thick yellow pad before him.

"Hey! You made it! Great!"

He half stood up to extend his hand.

Brianna took it, smiling quietly to herself. All radio talk-show people must go to the same school. Be friendly, they must be advised, be up on your subject, and don't, by all means, offend your guests before you have them on the air—where they can't do very much to defend themselves because *you* have the power of the switch. It was just as well that over the past few weeks she had learned to deal with on-air interviews and could handle just about any question that anyone could ask. She felt confident about this session tonight.

"Yes," she answered in return. "Just in time."

"Great...great!" The man retook his seat. Then he said not another word for the next ten minutes, just continued to write on his pad and glance at the large clock that was positioned on the wall a little to Brianna's right.

Brianna contented herself with watching the men in the control room as they went about the business of keeping the station on the air.

Finally, Jason Daily looked up again and said, "We'll be on in about five minutes. The guys doing the news are just about done."

"All right," Brianna replied. A bevy of nervous

butterflies took flight, but they were less than the squadrons that used to appear when she first started doing this.

Her interviewer placed the earphones on his head, adjusted them to fit properly, then became still for a few minutes as he listened.

Then, "Okay... now," he said softly, causing a few of her butterflies to give a startled leap.

In a smooth, deep voice he made the introductions, telling his listeners who he was, who she was, what she did for a living, that she was in town to promote her latest book, and that the telephone lines would be open the last twenty minutes of the show for calls. Then they went to a commercial and Brianna gave a sigh.

Jason Daily's small eyes came to rest on her. "You have a chance to see the afternoon paper?" he asked, completely, as far as she could see, out of the blue.

"Er—no, I haven't."

The man's smile fell into a position Brianna could only describe as crafty.

"Should I have?" she asked.

"I guess you could say you might be interested," he replied mysteriously. That was all he had time to say before the commercial ended and he was again repeating some of what he had already said so that late tuners would know what was taking place.

For the first half of the show, the interview could have been done in her sleep: The same questions were asked city after city; she gave the same replies. It was only as the session progressed into the last half hour of exchange dialogue that the atmosphere seemed to change. Where before Jason Daily was a friendly, fatherly sort, interested in how she had accomplished what she had at such an early age, he now seemed to have mentally sharpened his teeth and transformed into another person.

"Tell me," he directed, that sly smile coming back onto his face, "when you write the kind of books you do, do you ever think about the people who read them? Take responsibility for the fact that they might act out some of the things you write about? I suppose I'm really referring to impressionable young teenagers. Should they read your books? And do you think their doing so increases the odds that they'll engage in promiscuous sex?"

Brianna stared at him flabbergasted! Good God! That was a new one—or rather an entire list of new ones! Her mind spun as it tried to find some sort of satisfactory answer.

"I don't believe people are influenced that much by what they read, Mr. Daily. I give them more credit than that."

"Who would you say read your books more, adults or young people?"

"Adults."

"Are they written for adults?"

Brianna's mouth felt tight, but she kept her smile firmly in place. Irritation was the emotion the man was striving to have her expose—and she wasn't going to give him the satisfaction of seeing it.

"Yes."

"But teen-agers do read them."

"Yes."

"And don't you feel responsible?"

"For what?"

"For contributing to the loss of morality this nation is suffering now. For the number of young girls who are going out and getting themselves pregnant."

Brianna's quick mind jumped at the opening he had given her. Drolly she returned, "I didn't know reading a book was the cause of pregnancy."

Now it was Jason Daily's turn to be irritated. Only he didn't have the presence of mind to disguise it. His next words were sharp, hostile.

"You know what I'm getting at. You put ideas in young people's heads—"

Brianna interrupted. "Any 'ideas' that you're referring to are already there. And their being there is only natural. If a young person is old enough to want to read one of my books, they already know the facts of life. Maybe what they're doing is searching for experience. And wouldn't you rather have them get their experience from the pages of a book rather than by trial and error in the backseat of some car?" She paused to take a breath but continued before he could form another comment. "I know what I write, Mr. Daily. And I'm not ashamed of it."

The man glared at her for besting him and quickly switched off to a commercial.

The tension in the small room was almost a physical presence during the minute they were off the air. Jason Daily's wounded pride didn't allow him to make

any effort to resume his friendly mien. Brianna knew
that he had only been baiting her, trying to pique interest in his show, up his ratings by bringing in a con-
troversial topic. But what had caused him to decide on
that subject with herself? Her books were explicit, but
not anywhere near objectionable for the greater mass
of people, otherwise her sales wouldn't be so great.
Neither would she be held in such warm regard by so
wide an array of readers, both young and old. Her
mind searched back over what had been said earlier,
looking for a clue. The only thing she could come up
with was his mention of a newspaper. Was that it?
Could there have been something in that day's paper
that could have sparked this attack?

Brianna's attention was brought back to her surroundings by the man's reintroduction to his show.
Again he repeated the telephone number of the station and prompted his listeners to call in and ask questions or give their opinions as to his quick summation
of their previous conversation. Almost before the
words left his mouth, the call lights on the telephone
at his side began to blink.

For the next twenty minutes Brianna was exposed
to both applause and debasement. But by far she came
out ahead. Fans and nonfans alike supported her
ideas—even some teen-agers called to tell San Antonio's favorite radio talk-show host (to hear him tell it)
that he was mistaken. And some of the people were
interested only in learning how they too could become successful writers.

Brianna left the station with her head held high. She

had again shaken hands with Jason Daily just to prove to him that she had class, and he had responded with another fatherly smile, to show that he had recovered his aplomb. When she had glanced into the control room over the host's shoulder, it was to see the two men inside smiling and giving her a thumbs-up sign. The resulting rush of justifiable pleasure stayed with her until she was able to stop at a nearby convenience store and purchase an afternoon paper.

Sitting in her car in the parking lot, under the artificial light of a street lamp, she soon found what she was looking for on the feature page. It was a piece with the heading "Cantrell's Corner," and beside it was a small picture of the man she had been trying so hard to keep out of her mind—Ryder Cantrell. He was smiling in that lazy way of his directly up into her eyes.

Brianna's fingers tightened onto the edges of the paper while a feeling of cold foreboding ground into a knot in the pit of her stomach. So that was who he was! A reporter! She should have known from the amount of questions he had asked. But she had been so involved in her physical reactions to him that she had barely noticed—and when she did, she had put it down to interest. How absolutely, positively, conceitedly stupid she had let herself be! And, dear Lord, what had she told him? Not once had she been on guard.

With growing dread her eyes scanned the first few sentences of the article and were immediately glued to it. It read:

Ah, romance! It happens every spring—or at least that's what the poets tell us—although the nurses at St. Stephen's would testify that it happens in the fall, in the winter, and in the summer as well. Their job is to care for unwed mothers who choose to have their babies rather than seek an abortion. And they should know.

But are we speaking of Romance here, in the pure sense of the word? Or are we referring to something else?

In the dictionary, romance is defined as: a tendency of the mind toward the wonderful and mysterious...something belonging rather to fiction than to everyday life. Yet is romance apart from everyday life? Not romance as the nurses at St. Stephen's or the local abortion clinics see it.

But how do other people understand it?—and let's leave out the poets; we already know their views. Instead, why don't we get into the head of someone who writes the stuff. A person who is preparing to visit our fine city to promote the publication of her newest book, *Wild Desert Flower*. How does she feel about "the heavenly experience"?

I met Brianna St. Clair quite by accident when I was taking care of some business in Dallas and she was at a bookstore holding court. She's young, 26; she's beautiful—fantastic blond hair with green eyes and a body that could make a man weep—and she's totally involved in her craft. And I do mean involved.

For hours I watched as women of all kinds, sizes, and ages lined up just for the honor of having her name written in their books. Then they happily trotted off to pay $3.95 plus tax. Ms. St. Clair was gracious throughout.

However, I wasn't interested in how our heroine acted with her public. I was curious how she would behave on a more elemental level. I guess you could say that I got my money's worth. Not that any money changed hands, I rush to assure you. But I do believe I found out more than I really wanted to know.

Ms. St. Clair is an interesting woman who accepts the ideals she writes about. I suppose if she didn't, she wouldn't be writing them. And she accepts them with a verve that can leave one breathless.

Oh, and just in case some of my regular readers fare wondering why I've included this seeming bit of fluff in a column usually devoted to higher ideas, let me reassure them that I haven't completely turned my back. I've written this as a public service, because, you see, Ms. St. Clair admitted to me that she uses people she knows as characters in her books. As an example: Look closely when you read *Wild Desert Flower*. (If you can get through its five hundred pages— although I must admit that I did and found it...interesting, as well.) See if you can find the person of a tavernkeeper who repeatedly tries to ravish one Dianna Muldoone, the lead character.

In reality the tavernkeeper is none other than Ms. St. Clair's father's employer who, Ms. St. Clair says, has lecherous intents—not only on herself but on her mother as well!

I can't help but wonder if Ms. St. Clair isn't guilty of a little too much fanciful thinking.

At any rate, watch out, San Antonio, she's arriving today and will be here for a few weeks to come.

By the time Brianna finished the article her fingers were crushing the paper. She couldn't believe what she had read. Slowly, and with more care, she read it again. And she still couldn't believe it. He had just as good as accused her of being the root cause of all teenage pregnancy problems—he hadn't said it, but it was implied. Then he had attacked her personally, said she held court! Snidely alluded to the price of her books as if she received most of the money herself—and didn't work for even the few pennies she did receive. Called it *stuff*! But worst of all, he had made it sound like she was some kind of lowlife! As if she had all the selectivity of a female dog in heat! As if she and he had— Brianna tried to control her rapidly pounding pulse, her erratic breathing, her burning temper. How dare he do that! He had been just as enthusiastic as she! At least at first. And he had had the nerve to print that about her father's boss. To hint that the situation might be a figment of her twisted imagination. What if her father found out? What would happen then? Didn't the man care? Or did he truly not believe her?

But did that matter? There it was, in black and white for all the world to see—or at least San Antonio. How was she supposed to live here for the next month or so? How would the people she met react to her?

With a great deal of difficulty Brianna forced herself to calm down. Her first inclination had been to go to the—she checked the top of the page for the newspaper's name—*The Sun* and demand a retraction. Raise all kinds of hell, threaten law suits.... But she wasn't sure on how firm a ground she stood legally. Then she hit upon the idea that might be her best method to counteract this—this—sophisticated libel. And that was to act as if it were all a joke. If she didn't let her anger and humiliation show, no one would wonder about its truth for long. She would take it in her stride. Yes, she concluded, that would be the best way. Pretending that a bully wasn't hurting you by laughing in his face sometimes got you into more immediate trouble, but the long-term effect was that he would eventually go away and leave you alone because no one likes to be laughed at—and, as well, when you were laughing, he could never be sure just how badly he was hurting you. Neither could anyone else who might be observing. So she would treat Ryder Cantrell and his article in just such a manner. And hope that everyone else would take her view and see the funny side. Then after accomplishing that, she would keep a low profile for a time—very low indeed.

Her hardest time was going to be tomorrow—she had the television interview. Brianna gave a soft little groan. That meant she was probably going to be called upon to defend herself in glorious, living color!

Brianna practiced setting the mental attitude that she hoped would carry her through, and when she used it on the bell captain at her hotel, she was encouraged by the returning smile he gave her.

The television interview was just as difficult in its own way as the radio show the evening before. But this time the fascination seemed to be with her use of people she knew as characters in her books. She supposed the other two subjects—promiscuity and her own loose morals—were too touchy a subject for such an early-morning show. And thankfully the woman questioning her did not even mention her father or his employer. With her false good humor very much in evidence, Brianna explained how she developed her characterizations, how she *sometimes* used acquaintances and friends as a *basis* for characters, but that in most instances the people who made up her books were purely imaginary, as were the situations.

From the television studio she went directly to her first signing. A larger than usual group of people were waiting for her, and throughout the day there seemed to be bigger crowds. In fact, each bookstore ran out of copies of her book long before she was scheduled to leave, but still the people did not stop coming. It seemed that they wanted to talk to her. And only a couple were a little strange: one asking her questions about the possibility of a publishing company being interested in the story of her life, and another holding a thick notebook of papers that he said were dictated to him by an alien being. But on the whole, the people were friendly, and interested, and curious to hear more of her views, as well as give their own. What she soon found was that she didn't have to pretend or act; people accepted her as she was. And that made her relax even more.

At the end of the day her only concern was that in some way the little article buried in the San Antonio paper could find its way to Pennsylvania and her father. But as she rested at a quiet table in the hotel bar, a glass of white wine held loosely in her fingers, she prodded herself into believing that it could never happen. It would be too much a quirk of fate.

However, the unexpected occurrences of the hours before did not in any way sweeten her thoughts concerning the cause of all her trouble. If he happened to walk into the bar right now and take a seat at her table, she would—

Her thoughts came to an abrupt stop as a long masculine form came to a halt across from her. Her green eyes flew upward, startled. No, it couldn't be! She hadn't conjured him up, had she?

She breathed a small sigh of relief when she saw that the man standing there was about the same age as herself, with bright carrot-red hair, freckles, and a pair of laughing brown eyes.

"Hi," he greeted her. "Are you Brianna St. Clair?"

Brianna gave a short nod.

"I thought so. I saw you on TV this morning. Mind if I share your table?"

"No." She made as if to pull away. "I was just going anyway."

His brown eyes lost their laughter and he had the look of a child deprived of a long-awaited pleasure.

"Ah, heck! You don't really have to leave, do you? I was wanting to talk with you. My wife's one of your biggest fans."

Brianna let her eyes follow the character lines on his face. Then she straightened her tired shoulders and settled back in her chair.

"No," she said softly. "I can stay for a while."

The smile was immediately back. "Good! Anna would never understand it if I told her we had met, but that I didn't get to say more than a word to you."

Brianna took a sip of her wine.

"Are you staying at this hotel?" he asked.

"Yes." After what had happened in Dallas she was a little leery of talking with strange men who appeared out of nowhere and started asking questions.

"You going to be in San Antonio long?"

"For a time."

"Hotels are hell to live in for very long. I know, because I've done it before."

She took the ball from his court.

"Are you staying here too?"

A wide grin showed even white teeth. "Heck no. Anna and I have a place on the north side. I'm in real estate."

Brianna's green eyes widened. "You are?"

"You bet! That's why I was asking if you have a place to go or if you're staying on here. I have a really neat little house that's just come onto the market and the terms are easy—"

"I'm not interested in buying, Mr. . . . ."

"Oh, I'm sorry. Daniels, Paul Daniels. And I didn't mean that either. It's up for rent."

After the last few days she had spent, Brianna's mind was becoming a little fuzzy. Or possibly it was the arrival of the wine on her empty stomach. She had not eaten anything since breakfast and that had only been a half slice of toasted English muffin and coffee.

"I'm sorry, I—"

"I'm offering it to you."

"You are?"

"Sure! And I bet I can make you a deal that you won't be able to refuse."

Brianna smiled. "What's wrong with it?"

Paul Daniels grinned back. "Oh, the roof doesn't leak, and all the plumbing works. It's just that the friend of mine who owns it isn't sure whether he wants to sell it or not. It's been in his family for years, but he's not married and lives in an apartment and, well"—he shrugged—"it's got a lot of memories for him, both good and bad."

"Where's it located?" If a great deal of her work was going to be done at the institute, which she knew was not too far from this hotel, she didn't want to have to travel across town to get back to it.

"Not far away. It's in the old King William District, just a hop and a skip from Hemisfair Plaza."

Hemisfair Plaza! That was where the institute was located!

Suddenly Brianna became more interested. "How much is he asking?"

Paul Daniels named a price that had her instantly agreeing. "If I can see it on approval first."

"Of course. But I'm not worried. I think you're going to fall in love with it."

"Maybe I will, but I still want to check it out first."

"All right. When would you like to go? Is tomorrow morning too early?"

"Not at all." Brianna gave a tired smile. "I'd say now, but I don't think I could keep my eyes open."

"Then tomorrow morning it is. I'll meet you here at ten. Okay?"

"That's fine."

Paul raised himself to his feet, his slender form unwinding from the table with graceful ease. "I don't think you're going to regret it."

Brianna only smiled. She was not about to totally commit herself.

Ten thirty the next morning found Brianna and Paul Daniels standing across from one of the most beautiful white stone Victorian houses she had seen in ages. In a way it could be termed small, at least in comparison to its imposing neighbors, but by no stretch of the imagination could it be termed "little." It was two storied with both an upstairs and downstairs recessed porch covering a little over half of the front exterior of the building. A double set of narrow arched windows decorated the extended rooms that made up the rest. A low carved wooden railing, painted white, enclosed the upper porch, and below, three carved arches graced the lower porch exterior. Completing the picture was a low stone fence topped with intricate wrought iron filigree and large sheltering oak trees that gave an abundance of shade while pink-flowering crepe myrtles lent color.

"Well, what do you think?" Paul asked at last.

"I'll take it," Brianna breathed, almost reverently.

"Without even seeing inside?" he laughed softly.

"Without even seeing inside."

"I told you you'd like it."

"And you were right." She looked about at the surrounding houses, all but a few kept in perfect condition. "What is this place?"

"The King William Historic District. It's listed in the National Historic Register. In the late nineteenth century this is where almost all the prosperous businessmen of the area lived."

"It's beautiful."

Paul let his gaze survey the street as well. "Well, it's not quite what it used to be—along the way it fell on hard times. But some private individuals have been trying to restore it. There's a mansion not far that way"—he motioned with his hand—"that's open for tours if you want to see what it looked like back then. A lot of old things, furniture and all."

Brianna followed the direction he was pointing and then looked back at the house.

"The man who owns this—why doesn't he live here?" She gave a short deprecating laugh. "I don't mean to be nosy, but if I owned anything so beautiful,

I wouldn't leave it and I definitely wouldn't rent it out."

Paul shrugged. "He has his reasons."

For a moment Brianna felt effectively put in her place, but Paul's cheerful grin soon got her back to her ease.

"Come on. Let's go inside. I never close a deal until I'm sure the lessee is satisfied."

Happily Brianna walked with him.

Inside, the home was even more beautiful. High graceful ceilings, a winding staircase—the owner had modernized with an eye to retaining the essence of the previous century while not sacrificing comfort. The house was furnished with a combination of antiques and collectibles yet at the same time held more current pieces that seemed to represent the best of several eras.

In all, the interior claimed ten rooms: three large bedrooms, two fully modernized baths, a large, roomy kitchen, and a beautifully added glass-enclosed patio where white lattice-work wood made a canopy that gave the onlooker the illusion of being totally out-of-doors. A profusion of hanging baskets and potted plants gave credence to this fancy.

When Paul saw Brianna looking at the healthy, well-cared-for plants, he explained, "The owner has a woman come in once a week to maintain the place."

The answer also explained another puzzling question that had earlier surfaced in Brianna's mind—that of the absence of any closed, musty smell.

"So, what do you think? You still want it?" Paul prompted.

Brianna knew she shouldn't agree; she would rattle around in a house this size like a loose marble in a tin can, but she couldn't make herself say no. As he had foreseen yesterday, she had instantly fallen in love with it; it appealed to every instinct within her that reached out for anything old.

"Definitely," she confirmed.

"Great!" Paul rubbed his hands together. "Let's go to my office and get the papers signed, and then—" He paused to raise a questioning eyebrow. "Would you like to come to my house and meet Anna? I told her I met you yesterday, and she was so excited. She told me to be sure to invite you to lunch. What do you say? Or do you have something else planned?"

Brianna could only shake her head. Paul reminded her strongly of a whirlwind. But she added, "I don't want to make a pest of myself."

"You're not a pest!" he contradicted. "Having you over to our house is an honor!"

At that Brianna started to laugh. Why was it when a person achieved some measure of success in their chosen field other people started to look upon them as something different? In reality they hadn't changed. They were still just as flawed, just as secure or insecure as the next person.

"Come on," Paul coaxed. "Anna's going to fix some of her famous spaghetti."

Brianna couldn't resist. "Oh, all right. Thank you. That sounds delicious." Then a sudden thought occurred. "I will be able to move in here tomorrow, won't I?"

"I don't see why not."

All the way to Paul's realty office Brianna's mind was busy with plans for the future. She would take tomorrow to settle in, go grocery shopping so that she would have something to eat, arrange for a telephone. That last thought again brought on a momentary attack of worry. She needed to call home later this evening, let her parents know she had found a place to stay, see if they had heard anything about the story Ryder Cantrell had written.

A sudden cloud of returning anger descended on Brianna's spirit. So far today she had been able to put the man and what he had done to her far away from her conscious thoughts. But like a bad penny, he seemed to have a way of returning. And with each time that he did, her anger increased. She began to wonder if she had done the right thing in not storming into his office to confront him face to face.

Yet, in a place deep down in her soul, Brianna was still smarting from the humiliation of his rejection. And she knew that it was best if she never saw him again.

The business aspect of signing the lease took only a few seconds. But the introductions in the office took longer. It seemed that his wife was not the only person Paul Daniels had been talking to.

When at last they were free, Paul smiled a little ruefully as he backed his car out of its parking space.

"Sorry about that. I guess I got a little carried away."

How could anyone be unhappy with Paul? He looked like nothing more than an overgrown little boy with his red hair and freckles, and that infectious smile.

"It's no problem. I didn't mind. I like talking to people."

For a moment Paul hesitated before easing the car forward. "You know, you're the first famous author I've met. Are they all like you?"

Brianna's soft mouth tilted up into an amused smile. "And how is that?"

"Nice—really and truly nice."

"I have three older brothers and one sister. And ever since we were children if one of us began to get a big head, someone else could always be counted on to bring the offender back to size."

"So it is just you."

Brianna hastened to correct him. "No. On a whole I've never known a group of people to be so warm and outgoing. And I've met quite a number—famous and not quite so famous. Although there always are a few who begin to believe they're God's gift to humanity. But I think you can find that kind of person in any field."

"My brother's a doctor. I know what you mean."

"Which category does he fit into?"

"The last. But then he's just twenty-eight. He hasn't been practicing for long."

"Doctors are a little different."

"Not when they're your brother," he corrected darkly and put the car into motion.

The house Paul stopped before was the exact opposite of the home Brianna had just signed her lease on. It was thoroughly modern in every aspect. Long smooth

lines, stained wood instead of rock and painted sur-
faces, a series of long narrow windows repeated twice
under a veeing arch. It was beautiful; yet it lacked
character. There were too many other houses just like
it—or at least a close rendition—lined up nearby. But
she was careful not to let her opinion show. Obviously
Paul was pleased, and that was all that mattered.

The young woman she was introduced to as Anna
came as more than a surprise to Brianna. At first she
had thought her to be merely a child. She was tiny-
boned, under five feet, with dark hair and great dark
eyes. And she was also very, very pregnant. About
eight months, Brianna's experienced eye, which was
gained from going through her sister's three pregnan-
cies, told her.

"I'm so glad you could come," Anna said, her
voice welcoming.

"Thank you for asking," Brianna returned, liking
the younger woman instantly.

"It's our pleasure," Anna said again a little formally, then winked at her husband, a gamine smile
lighting up her face. "Paul's, mine, and we're not
quite sure who yet."

"Oh, yes, we are," Paul spoke up. "What you see
there, Brianna, is another little Paul in the making."

"My mother says it's a girl," Anna teased, her dark
eyes bright.

"And mine says it's a boy. She did that string test,
or whatever."

"Mine can tell from the way I'm carrying it."

"Very scientific," Brianna murmured, joining in

with their fun. "I hope no one is going to be disappointed."

"Are you kidding? This kid is the first grandchild on either side of the family—they'll take it even if it comes out bright green!"

"Or with red hair and freckles," Anna grinned and then scooted quickly away from her husband's reach. "I think I'd better check the sauce. Paul, see if Brianna would like anything to drink."

Brianna witnessed Paul's expression as he watched his wife, who still managed to be very graceful even in her advanced state of near motherhood, move from the room. She could see all the love, all the caring, and her throat tightened.

Finally when Anna had completely disappeared, Paul turned to her. His eyes were alive with warm emotion.

"She's very beautiful, Paul," Brianna said softly.

"Yes, she is."

"When is the baby due?"

"Three weeks from today. Er, would you like anything to drink? We have wine to go with the spaghetti, but I can probably filch some before if you'd like."

"No. I'm fine. I'd rather wait."

All at once Paul became aware that they were still standing where they had been since first entering the room.

"Hey, I'm sorry. Sit down, please. You probably think us the rudest people alive. But when we have friends over, we expect them to make themselves at home. To get comfortable, relax."

Brianna was doing just as he directed when Anna came back into the room.

"Another minute or two and it will all be ready. Are you very hungry, Brianna?"

"Well, actually, yes. I suppose I could lie and say only a little, but—"

"Your parents taught you not to tell lies on such short acquaintance," Paul finished for her, then grinned. "It's a good thing you didn't...and that you are. Anna always makes enough to feed an army!"

"Then I won't feel bad asking for seconds."

"Definitely not. Or thirds either."

Brianna gave an amused chuckle. "I didn't say I was *that* hungry!"

A buzzer coming from the area where Anna had just emerged called her back. "I'll get that, you rest," Paul volunteered. "I'll call when it's time for you both to come."

He paused only to see Anna to a seat on the long sofa before hurrying to quiet the summons.

"The man exaggerates, but he's pretty special," Anna confided woman to woman.

"I can tell."

"Can you?" Anna seemed a little surprised.

"Of course."

A little frown wrinkled the skin of Anna's brow. "My parents didn't want me to marry him. They had a nice Italian boy all picked out. Sometimes I'm still not quite sure if they totally accept him."

"Maybe the baby will help."

"I think it already has. We've only been married

nine months—and to my father, any man who's that fertile can't be all bad.''

Brianna laughed at Anna's wry aside. Then before there was time for her to say anything in response, Paul had stuck his head into the room and called, "First notice! If you don't get here soon I'm going to eat it all."

Anna struggled a bit heavily to her feet. "Don't you just love the way he requests our presence formally?"

All through the meal a warm banter was exchanged, causing Brianna to experience a shade of loneliness. That was the way she and her brothers and sister always enjoyed each other's presence. It had been so long since they had been together! But as time wore on, she soon became completely caught up in the lighthearted exchanges and when the meal was done, felt as close to these newfound friends as she did many of her older ones.

Brianna's offer to help with the clean up of the dishes was accepted gratefully, which had her feeling all the more close to these people.

It was strange, she reflected as she arranged a rinsed plate in position in the dishwasher, but sometimes you could know a person for years and yet not really feel close. And yet others, you could meet and an instant affinity would spring up between you.

Just the way it happened between me and Ryder Cantrell!

The second the thought fought its way into her consciousness, Brianna tried to bury it. Why did she have to keep thinking about the man? Hadn't she learned her lesson? There was no affinity between them. It had only been a product of her imagination. He had played her along, used her, in more ways than one, and she, like a fool, had let him.

"Brianna?" Anna's concerned voice prompted her to look across at her. "Are you all right?"

Brianna's green eyes finished the job of coming back into focus. She looked down at the plate she had kept hold of, and quickly let go. "Yes, yes, I'm fine."

Anna's dark gaze concentrated on her. "Are you sure? You just kind of turned off... like you were in another world."

"Oh!" Now what did she say? "I—I suppose I was."

"Is that how you get ideas for your books? Do they just kind of hit you?"

"Sometimes." Brianna thankfully accepted the excuse, and another plate.

Anna sighed, "It must be wonderful being able to write, to create such fascinating worlds."

Paul, who had been listening to their conversation as he transferred the still heaping bowl of spaghetti into a large container for refrigeration, said, "It's probably a devil of a lot of work as well."

Brianna smiled. "It's both."

"And you wouldn't trade what you do for the world."

Her green eyes met his sparkling brown. "No. Not for anything."

The hours of the afternoon passed so quickly that Brianna was shocked to look down at her wristwatch and see that it was nearly five.

"Good heavens! I can't believe it!" she cried.

"What? What?" Paul put his can of Lite beer down on a coaster, the gentle breeze that found its way into the backyard ruffling his hair.

"I've got to go! I didn't mean to stay here all afternoon."

"Is that some kind of crime?"

"No, but—"

"Well, you can't leave until Anna wakes up. So relax."

Brianna glanced toward the small figure lying curled on her side in the arms of a stationary hammock.

"But what about your work?"

"I needed some time off."

Brianna's lips turned up. "And any excuse would do."

"Naturally!" Paul leaned back in his chair and pretended to close his eyes. Instead he was watching her through the slits. "And you don't look any worse for resting a little yourself."

"No—"

"So like I said, relax some more. Enjoy it."

"Is that some sort of prescription?"

"Yes. Being the brother of a doctor makes me qualified."

"Just like being the sister of a steelworker makes me able to construct a building."

"Exactly."

Brianna tilted her head. "Paul? Has anyone ever told you you're perfect bait for the little men in white coats?"

Paul chuckled. "Every day."

"So it doesn't bother you now?"

"Nope!"

Brianna was about to make another choice observation when she saw Paul's eyes widen at something behind her back. Whatever it was made him sit promptly forward.

Impelled by both curiosity and his mild alarm, she turned to see what he was looking at.

Then she wished that she had not. All the breath whooshed from her lungs while she felt as if she had been hit hard in the region of her stomach. Her mind began to spin dizzily, refusing to function on anything more difficult than its unconscious duties, and her face went totally white.

"Ryder! What are you doing here?" Paul demanded, anxiety coloring his words as he glanced quickly at Brianna.

Ryder Cantrell hesitated for a moment, as if he too had been caught off guard by Brianna's presence. Then a cool assurance seemed to reclaim his body and that slow lazy smile pulled at his lips.

"Well, I did knock," he drawled, his deep blue eyes lighted by a mocking laughter, coming to rest on Brianna as well. "Hello, Brianna. How's life been treating you?"

Chapter Four

"Hello, Brianna. How's life been treating you?" The words hung in the air.

Brianna could say nothing. This wasn't real! It wasn't really happening! Ryder Cantrell wasn't standing there looking at her as if for all the world they had last parted with little more than a calm good-bye.

Paul had come up out of his chair. "I thought you were still in Dallas!"

"Obviously I came back."

He sauntered closer to them. Brianna could not take her eyes away. Ryder paused beside Anna and bent to sweep a fly-away strand of black hair back into place beside her cheek. Anna stirred slightly but did not awaken.

"When did you get in?" Paul's throat sounded tight.

"About an hour ago." Ryder straightened.

"You should have called."

"Why? I've never needed to before."

"Well, because..." Paul looked guiltily back toward Brianna.

Brianna's senses were slowly returning to normal. She could tell herself that Ryder wasn't here, that he wasn't standing close enough for her to reach out a hand to touch, but it wouldn't be true. And she was painfully coming to admit that fact.

Her eyes were dark with remaining disbelief when she met Paul's worried gaze.

"Because of your company?" Ryder finished for him. Brianna's attention snapped to center fully on him, and her heart skipped as he took the step that separated them. "You know that we've already met."

Paul seemed to have suddenly come to an absence of words. He stood mutely as Ryder leaned over to reach out and tip Brianna's chin further upward until she was compelled to meet his eyes.

"Haven't we?" he prompted, his voice huskily sexy.

Through the clamor of conflicting instincts, one emotion emerged superior. Again Brianna's eyes darkened, but this time it was not from shock. This time it was from anger.

She jerked her chin away from his hold and spat, "Yes—to my regret!"

Ryder had the audacity to smile and whistle softly. "Whew. The lady isn't pleased."

If she could have somehow gained the physical ability to knock him to the ground and then grind him into dust with the heel of her shoe, she would have done it. But since that was an impossibility, her hands tightened their grip on the aluminum arms of the lawn chair, and she contented herself with saying acidly, "You know what you can do, Mr. Cantrell. You can go straight to hell and—"

Brianna had not been watching the level of her voice, and as a result, Anna was beginning to struggle to sit up.

"What's going on?" she asked groggily. She rubbed a hand across her eyes and then drew a short breath when she saw that Ryder was there. "Oh! Oh, no!"

Ryder transferred his amused gaze to her. "Cripes, with the kind of welcome I've been getting I should have stayed away."

His dry response made Anna blush. "Oh, Ryder, you know you're always welcome here, but—" Her color deepened even more under Brianna's accusing stare.

So it had all been another false scene! She had thought she found friends again, and in reality they were not. All along they had known Ryder, known what he had done to her.

Brianna stood up on legs that were trembling from her fury. Coldly she began, "It was very nice meeting you both. Thank you for lunch. Now, if I could use your telephone..."

"What for?" Paul questioned quickly.

"To call a taxi."

"Oh, Brianna, don't. Please don't!" Anna rocked, trying to gain her feet, her small face crumpled with regret and worry.

Paul rushed over to help his wife, his arm coming around to encircle her shoulders as she wavered while trying to get her balance.

The next thing Brianna knew Ryder's lips were moving close to her ear. It seemed as if a thousand rabbits ran over her skin as she stiffened, but when she heard his words, she froze a little on the inside as well.

"Anna doesn't need this. She's been having a hard enough time with this pregnancy. If you don't want the baby to be born early, then don't make a fuss!"

Brianna remained stiff. Yet she could see the truth of his words. Anna did look deeply shaken.

"I'll take you back," Ryder volunteered in a more normal voice. "I think we need to have a little talk."

"Yes, Ryder, please do," Anna pleaded, her large dark eyes melting. "And, Brianna, we didn't mean—"

Paul interrupted her sentence. "Let Ryder handle it, sweetheart."

Brianna turned away, her back straight. She would create no upheaval here, but she still couldn't act as if everything were on the same footing as it had been before. It wasn't. She felt betrayed.

The small entourage moved silently through the house, where Brianna collected her purse before moving on to the outdoors. A familiar black car sat in the driveway.

For a moment she was tempted to hold out for the taxi, insist on calling one, but Anna looked as if she was about to cry, and Brianna found that she couldn't do it. At least she would let Ryder drive her out of sight. Then she would walk until she found a phone. And there would be nothing he could do about it!

He opened the door for her, and she slipped aloofly

inside. She kept her face turned away from the couple standing silently at their door; she didn't want to see their faces.

The muffled roar of the car's engine was the only sound inflicting itself on the ears of the two people within as it was first reversed and then shifted forward. Brianna was determined not to say anything, at least not until she was ready to be let out—which wouldn't be long considering the speed at which Ryder was driving. And Ryder looked as if his face was carved from stone, so hard was it set.

Then two things happened: Ryder suddenly reduced his speed, as if realizing that they were in a residential neighborhood, and following that, a series of short, clipped words broke through the stiffness of his lips.

"Well, are you proud of yourself?"

Brianna's head swung quickly about, this time to stare at him incredulously.

"Me?" she questioned. How in God's name could he ask that of her? She should be the one asking him— as well as giving him a few very well thought out, pointed opinions!

"Yes, you!" His blue eyes shifted momentarily to her from the street. "You made Anna and Paul feel like worms."

"I did?" Words tumbled in her mind, but she seemed unable to voice them coherently.

"Especially after I told you about Anna's problems with the baby."

Suddenly everything came together for Brianna,

and she demanded tightly, "Don't you think you should have thought of that earlier? *I'm* not responsible for how those people feel. *You* are! They're your friends after all—"

"That's right, they are," he interrupted.

"So don't try to shift the blame!"

"I didn't behave like a spoiled brat!"

"Neither did I!"

"That, my dear, is a matter of opinion."

Brianna's eyes were flashing sparks of emerald flame. But she controlled her tongue. It was no use! The man would never listen! And why the hell should she be trying to justify herself anyway? None of this was her doing—she had been the one deceived.

Her hand went to the handle of the door.

"Let me out. Let me out right here. I told you I wanted to get a taxi, and I still do." Her voice was shaking slightly from the strength of her anger.

"And you think you're going to find one here?"

"I don't really care."

"No."

"What?"

"I said, no."

"Stop the car, Ryder!"

His answer was a deeper touch on the accelerator. They were nearing the outskirts of the subdivision and the freeway was only yards away.

Brianna saw that her only hope was the traffic light positioned on the corner. It was turning yellow now; he would have to stop. Her body tensed.

But as if he had read her mind, when the car

slowed, one of his hands moved from the steering wheel to her arm, holding her firmly, yet not too tightly, just where she was.

Brianna tried to shake the unwanted pressure away, and brought her other hand up to pry at the restraining fingers. Yet she was unable to loosen his grip, and she gave a low, furious moan.

She was not set free until they were safely traveling at speed. Just as a point of exaggeration, Brianna rubbed her arm as if it had been badly hurt. In truth, it had not, but she didn't want him to come away from the incident too lightly. Let him think he had hurt her; let it prick at his conscience—that is, if he had one!

"Did that make you feel like all-powerful man?" she asked harshly. "Keep the little woman in her place with a show of superior strength?"

Ryder didn't seem to be stung by her words as she had wanted. "It was either that or run the red light," he replied. "And I didn't relish either getting a ticket or taking the chance of getting us killed."

"You could have let me go!" Brianna stormed.

"That would have been too easy."

"Too easy?"

"I told you we need to talk." As he said this, he looked back over his left shoulder to gauge the flow of traffic as they mounted a freeway entrance ramp. Brianna saw that his attention was away from her for this moment and again put her hand to the door handle.

Whether she truly meant to open it and jump, she was never really sure, because she had no chance to act. Ryder glanced around again, saw what she was about to do, and with a split second reaction, jerked at her arm—this time bruising it.

"What the hell were you trying to do?" he demanded with harsh anger after he had righted the car from the drunken swerve it had taken. "Commit suicide?"

"It would be better than talking with you!" she spat back in return, smarting in more ways than one. Suicide had been the farthest thing from her mind, and when the car had wavered so wildly as he reached over to prevent her possible escape, she had been afraid that she might be the cause of a horrible accident. But she wasn't about to let him know how shaken she was!

"I'm sorry you feel that way, but it's going to happen."

"It takes two people to talk!"

"No," he contradicted. "It takes one to talk and one to listen."

"And I'm supposed to be the one who listens."

"You've got that right."

Slowly Brianna's agitation was lessening, and she could tell from the unconscious lightening of his grip on her arm that he was relaxing a little again as well. Finally he took his hand away all together.

Yet he warned, "Don't try that again, or..."

"Or what?" she asked as he paused.

"Or I'll make you regret it."

"What will you do?" Brianna challenged, tipping her head as if truly wanting to know. "Beat me to within an inch of my life? Boil me in oil? Tie me to a rack and laugh as my bones are pulled from their sockets?''

Her sarcasm rolled off of him like water on a bird's wing. In fact, his features mellowed enough to fall into an appreciative smile.

"You really do have an active imagination."

"Thank you!" Brianna directed her face forward and contained the impulse to grind her teeth. Really, the man was just too much!

Without her being aware of it, the miles the sports car traveled passed quickly. She was barely conscious of when they pulled off the freeway and turned onto a street that led downtown. Instead, her mind was filled with trying to find ways she could strike out at him, reviewing all the charges she had against him.

When the car pulled to a stop, it took Brianna a moment to realize that their motion had ceased. She blinked her eyes as she looked about them.

"Where are we?" she asked, screwing up the skin of her forehead.

"Have you ever heard of the Alamo?"

Brianna smiled sweetly. Of course she had heard of the place where the small band of Texans had fought for days to hold off the Mexican Army in one of the most important battles of the Texas War for Independence—and where they had all died.

"Of course. Who hasn't?"

"Do you know what it looks like?"

"I've seen pictures."

"That's the real thing over there," he motioned. "Do you want to go look around?"

Brianna's head swiveled to her right. She wasn't sure what she had expected. She had seen pictures and it did look like them, yet something was wrong. The white two-story structure looked old, its architecture that of a Spanish mission, which she knew it once was: a set of massive twin doors set well back beneath a wide arch, pillars carved of stone positioned on either side of the doors, a roof line that was flat on the ends, building to a rounded swell on top directly over the front entrance.

Then as her eyes ran over it again, all at once she realized what the difference was—the Alamo was surrounded by the inner city; tall, modern buildings were only a few steps away. In her mind she had always pictured the historic building off somewhere alone. But from the stream of visitors going in and out, that fact didn't seem to bother them... and after a moment it didn't bother her either. The mission had been here first; the city had just mushroomed around it, which was the way of things. At least the monument had been preserved.

"Well?" Ryder prompted.

Brianna switched her thoughts to the more immediate present. She knew what Ryder was up to. He wanted to talk, and he thought she would be more amenable to listening if he plied her with a liberal slice of Texas history. He had done it before, at the inn. He had used her love of things old to loosen her tongue. But this time her tongue was muted, just as her ears were closed. She didn't want to hear his explanations. Yet she would like to see inside, go with the rest of the visitors. So why shouldn't she? she suddenly asked herself. In order that this afternoon not be a total loss, why shouldn't she take advantage of the opportunity and let him guide her through? Use *him* for a change.

"Okay," she agreed with a quick, crisp nod.

Ryder's blue eyes narrowed suspiciously on her features.

"That was easy," he murmured. And when she said nothing, added, "Maybe a little too easy. What are you up to?"

"I'm not up to anything," Brianna answered smoothly. "I want to see the mission, that's all."

"But you aren't prepared to talk."

Brianna felt a lashing of consternation, however she didn't let it show.

"You said my part was to listen," she reminded him.

His lazy smile appeared. "That I did, but I didn't expect you to limit yourself to doing just that."

"You think you know me so well?"

"No," he grinned, and her stomach tightened as an awareness of his physical appeal returned to her. "You have a habit of keeping me guessing."

Good! she thought. *And I'll be sure to continue—as long as it takes to get rid of you.*

Two hours later Brianna and Ryder had seen everything there was to see at the museum, which was what it was, with a touch of commercial entrepreneurship thrown in. Somehow the blending did not sit well with

Brianna, but when Ryder assured her that the selling of tourist items provided the area's upkeep, she was satisfied to a degree, with only a small stubborn part of her still rebelling because it seemed so disrespectful to the men who had given their lives there. But at least the commercial side of the operation was out of the main portion of the Alamo, enclosed in a nearby building. That fact helped a little.

"How did you like it?" Ryder asked as they walked in a side courtyard where a huge oak tree's great breadth gave shade to most of the area.

Brianna was cautious. All through the tour Ryder had made no attempt to touch on anything but what they were seeing. And, to her chagrin, she found that he was amazingly well informed.

"It was very interesting," she admitted coolly.

"Could you use some of it in a book?"

Brianna stiffened. "Possibly."

Ryder stuffed his hands into the front pockets of his camel-colored slacks and sighed. "This can't be put off much longer. Come on. Let's sit over there." He directed her attention to a small cement bench beside a stone archway that led to the front plaza.

Brianna went, but it was not with total willingness. She still was determined not to absorb anything he had to say, but the small nagging fear that her own curious nature was going to betray her had begun to grow. And her suspicion sharpened when Ryder started off by totally disconcerting her.

"I've changed my mind," he stated easily. "I want to hear what you're thinking."

"About what?"

"About everything."

"What everything?"

"Brianna—"

At that Brianna shed her shell of pretended obtuseness. If he was determined to give her the first option to make a thrust, then he definitely was not going to be disappointed. Her attempt at cool indifference went the way of the wind and a resumption of her previous anger took its place.

"All right!" she flashed. "I'll play it your way. Just who the hell do you think you are? What you did has got to be one of the most unethical, immoral displays of irresponsibility I have ever seen in my entire life! You didn't tell me who you were. You got all kinds of information out of me. Then you printed it!" Brianna took a quick breath. "I've never liked giving interviews because too many times newspeople never bother to check their facts. They scrupulously write down what you say, then when it comes time to compose the story, they must find that they can't read their own writing! I can't tell you the number of inaccuracies that have gone into print about me!"

"Was I inaccurate?" he asked softly.

Brianna's mouth tightened. "No. What did you do? Tape record our conversations?"

"I have a good memory."

"Too good for your own good!" Brianna retorted. "You realize, of course, that I'm definitely thinking about suing you and your newspaper."

"What for?"

"For defamation of character!" She clung to the first reason that came into her mind.

"And exactly how did I defame you?"

"You practically told the world that I'm some kind of—of—" She needed her thesaurus. *Slut* was the word that slid first to her tongue, but she didn't want to use it.

"No, I didn't." He grasped her unstated meaning.

"Oh, yes, you did!"

"I just wrote that you had the morals of your books. Is there something wrong with that? I've been told that on the radio show you said you weren't ashamed of what you put in your books. Was that a lie?"

"No!"

"Then what's to be upset about?"

Plenty! Brianna thought furiously. Especially when he had intimated that they had slept together. But she wasn't about to bring that subject up. So she changed course a little.

"You included something I told you in confidence in your sleazy little article!"

"Watch it! It wasn't sleazy."

"That, my dear," she echoed, "is a matter of opinion."

"Touché," he murmured with a touch of humor.

Brianna ignored him. "You wrote what I said about my father's employer—do you know what problems that could create if it ever gets back to him?"

"It won't. My column's not syndicated. It's just a little local thing."

"Can you guarantee that?"

"Practically."

"Aha! You can't."

"No, but I almost can. Anyway, I said I thought it was a part of your imagination."

"And that's another thing. You made me look like some kind of blathering idiot!"

"People draw what they want from a column like mine."

"I still say you were unethical in the extreme to betray a confidence."

"So you're still on to that."

"Yes!"

"It wasn't a confidence."

"It was!"

"No." He shook his dark head. "You told me voluntarily, and when I said that it would make a good story, you agreed. That was giving me permission, in case you didn't know. And not once did you say that anything you were telling me was off the record. So not by anyone's standards could what I did be called unethical."

Brianna's fists curled into tight little balls. It was all she could do not to strike out at that nose of his and hope that she drew blood.

"But I didn't know you were a reporter!" she said through clenched teeth.

"Did it matter? You didn't hesitate a second when you told me, so I decided that if you didn't mind if the world knew, you wouldn't mind if I helped you along by making the information a matter of public record."

"It mattered!"

"Again, are you ashamed? Most writers use people they know to form their characters, whether consciously or unconsciously—a kind of kaleidoscope of faces, names, and mannerisms."

"You have an answer for everything, don't you?"

"No."

"The hell you don't!"

"This conversation is degenerating."

"You started it!"

"And now I'm going to finish it." He leaned close to her, trapping her with his sudden intentness. "You've had your turn, now you're going to listen to me." He paused for only a second, as if collecting his ammunition. "I don't really care what you think about me. Man for man I probably have more enemies in this town than friends. So one more won't make me or break me. What I do care about is Anna and Paul. And how you react to them. They're good people, Brianna. They haven't done anything to hurt you. So don't you hurt them...especially Anna. All I asked them to do was help you. I thought that was the least I could do since—"

"Guilty conscious?" she interjected.

"No. I didn't do anything that I'd feel guilty about. I stopped when I started to feel bad about myself, remember?"

Brianna's face flooded with color. So that was what his withdrawal had been about. He had started to feel bad about himself! Well, good for him! Now, how was that supposed to make her feel? Grateful to him?

"I told you I'd send someone over to help you find

a place to stay while you were in San Antonio—and Paul was that person.''

"Don't tell me you bother to keep your word."

"I try to."

Brianna snorted disbelievingly, showing her contempt for all that he had said over the last fifteen minutes.

Ryder shrugged. "Believe what you want." Left unspoken was the added thought, *I don't really care.* "But don't have hard feelings about the Daniels."

When Brianna remained stubbornly silent, Ryder ran a hand through his hair in exasperation and then got to his feet. "Come on. I'll take you to your hotel."

"No, thank you."

"I said I would."

"And I'm saying I don't want you to. I'd rather walk."

He cocked his head and examined her. "It's a long walk."

"I don't mind long walks."

"It might be dark before you get there."

"I don't mind the dark."

"What about the devils that inhabit the night?"

"Some devils are preferable to others."

"Meaning me."

"You said it; I didn't."

"You didn't have to." He gave another glance at the late evening sky. "You'll probably have time, if you don't get lost."

"Good-bye, Mr. Cantrell," she said pointedly.

"Good-bye, Brianna."

In spite of herself, when he said her name, she experienced a sweet chill. No one had ever said her name in just such a way—and no one probably ever would again. As she watched him walk away, she wondered if he had any idea that she wasn't quite the person he thought her to be.

The walk did prove to be an extended one, and she did get a little off course a couple of times, having to pause and ask directions. But she eventually found her way and gratefully fell into a tub of warm, fragrant water in order to relax and cool off. Even though it was September, the temperature was still extremely warm.

As she lay in the tub, Brianna tried to clear her mind of everything that had happened that day. But she was not very successful. The strong, rugged face of Ryder Cantrell, not to mention his forceful personality, seemed to attack her in a constant blitz, and she finally had to give up and step from the water, hoping that once she was able to keep herself occupied with ordering her dinner and then eating it, she would be able to escape from his dominion. However, even in that she could not completely expel him from her thoughts.

At last, beaten, she curled up on the edge of the couch and let her wayward thoughts have their way.

She had confronted him—at least she had been forced to confront him—and what good had it done her? He seemed to have a defense for everything. To his mind, he had done no wrong. And, hateful as it was for her to admit, she had freely given him all the information he had culled. Of course she had had no idea that he was a member of the media—but she should have learned long ago that if she didn't want a fact known, especially something as private as her family's dealings with Mr. Thornton, then she shouldn't have said it. But that was another of her faults—she was open in the extreme. If someone asked a question, she had a hard time not giving a direct answer. She had not been schooled in evasion. But this was the first time one of her unedited replies could have the possibility of hurting someone else, someone she loved. And she wasn't sure if she would ever be able to forgive Ryder Cantrell for exposing her to this worry—even if it had been mostly her fault. He had used what she said; *he* should have thought! Yet, she squirmed miserably on the cushion, was it his job to think, at least about something that should have been of great concern to her? Wasn't that her responsibility?

Responsibility! Brianna stiffened. She had been so wrapped up with everything else, she had forgotten to challenge him on his intimation that her books were somehow linked to the ruin of Western Civilization. But maybe that was just as well. As she remembered the wording of his column, he would only deny that he had done it, saying that he had only written about romance and poets and clinics, and people had jumped to their own conclusions.

Brianna breathed a long, tired sigh. This day had been interminable. Her only consolation was that she had found a house— Her mind stopped short. What was she going to do about the house? Did she keep it?

Immediately her thoughts swung to Paul and Anna. Were they innocents as Ryder had said? Had they only been trying to help her? She wanted to believe that. She had thought them to be such nice people! She wanted to be able to like them. Was it possible that they hadn't betrayed her? But she couldn't get beyond the fact that they knew Ryder, were his friends.

Then all at once Brianna didn't care anymore. Of this entire mess, the house stood out like a beacon of hope. It would be a beautiful place to stay while she was here—and be damned to the reasons behind why she had been directed to it. And be damned to Ryder Cantrell. Once before she had made the decision to erase his presence from her life. She was going to do it again.

There was only one thing left to check up on and then she could free herself of any thoughts of him by concentrating on her work.

The nearness of the ringing telephone in her ear sounded as if she could be calling the room next door; the same was true of the feminine voice who answered.

"Sylvia?" Brianna guessed.

"Bri?"

Brianna held the telephone closer. "Yes," she said, laughing shakily, all at once overcome by a feeling of homesickness. She didn't live with her parents, and her sister and brothers all had lives of their own, but they were still a closely knit unit and hearing her sister's voice over the miles made distance and time seem greater.

"Oh, Bri! How are you? Aren't you just about done? Are you still planning on staying in Texas for a while?"

The barrage of questions gave Brianna time to collect herself. For a moment, she was tempted to chuck everything—get on the quickest available jet and shoot through the sky back to Pennsylvania—but another side to her personality, the stubborn, determined side, shied away from that idea. As Ryder had said, running away would be too easy. Again Brianna wrested his name from her consciousness.

"Yes, I'm still in Texas, and yes, I'm going to stay here for a while. I just took a lease out on a place today. You'd love it, Sylvia. It's small, Victorian."

"When can I come visit?"

"Whenever you want."

"You don't think I'm serious!"

"Are you?" Brianna pictured her sister. The oldest in the family, Sylvia barely looked her thirty-nine years. Rather on the small side too, she was a St. Clair blonde, but her eyes were like their mother's—a warm golden brown that grew even warmer when she smiled.

"No, you know I can't leave the kids."

"Mom and Dad would be glad to take them for a few days."

"I think you'd better talk to Mom before you volunteer her. Tommy Junior just got through showing them an experiment from his chemistry set, and the living room isn't going to be the same for weeks. Lord, the smell!''

Brianna laughed. ''They did survive us, you know,'' she reminded her sister.

''Yes, so they've earned their rest. And my crew is definitely not rest material.'' She paused. ''Do you want to talk with Mom? She's just gone out to the garage with Tom. She's going to show him how to splice a wire connection. We have a lamp at home with a bad gizmo at the top, where the light bulb screws on, and Tom's decided he wants to repair it himself this time. And who better to ask than Mom?''

Who better, was correct. Their mother was a genius with anything electrical—the complete opposite of their father, who would rather throw out a broken appliance than mess with its innards.

''No, it's not necessary. I just called to let you know I'm still alive.''

''You haven't been swept off your feet by any handsome cowboys yet, have you?'' her sister teased.

Brianna's answering laugh was a little strained. Cowboy? No. Newsman? Well, maybe. Impatiently she shook her head. *No! The answer was no!*

''I haven't seen any cowboys.'' She took refuge in making a reply.

''You haven't? I thought Texas was crawling with them.''

''I don't think they live in the cities, and that's the only places I've been.''

''Then get out into the countryside, my dear. If I

ever get to have a brother-in-law from you, I'd like
for him to have a Texas drawl."

To herself Brianna muttered: *They all have drawls
down here; he wouldn't necessarily have to be a cowboy.*

Then disgusted with herself and her crazy thought
processes, she engineered a change of subject. But she
had to be careful, she didn't want to make it sound as
if she was unduly concerned about anything.

"Is Dad all right?"

"Right as ever. He's got Patty on his lap now, rock-
ing her to sleep. I think she wore him out asking questions."

Brianna's three-year-old niece never seemed to tire
of doing that. To her, the world was a wonderland of
undiscovered answers.

"No problems with Mr. Thornton?"

Brianna could hear Sylvia's sigh. Her sister knew of
the man's predilection to proposition, but was a participant in keeping the information from her father.

With the level of her voice lower, she confided,
"The man's still a total s.o.b., but everything's under
control."

Brianna gave a soft relieved exhalation. As Ryder
had promised, the column had not left the area.

"I won't keep you, Sylvia. Kiss Mom and Dad for
me and tell your family hello."

"I will."

"I'll let you know my address and phone number
when I get it."

"Okay. Take care."

As Brianna slowly replaced the instrument she sank

back against the rear cushion of the couch. Well, it was done. Now she could go on with her life.

And to prove this, before she crawled into bed that night, she gathered all of her possessions and set her suitcases beside the door in preparation for her move tomorrow. The only exceptions were the clothing she was to wear and her overnight case, which contained her toiletries and makeup.

Then all she had to do was wait for sleep.

Which was a long time in coming.

Because everytime she began to relax, a lazy smile and a pair of laughing blue eyes appeared out of no-where to mock and disturb her.

Chapter Five

Early the next morning Brianna checked out of the hotel, eager to get settled in her new home. By noon, she was. There was no cleaning to be done; the place was totally spotless—not even a mote of dust on anything—and all she had to do was choose the room she was going to sleep in, unpack, and pay a visit to the nearest grocery store.

So with time to spare she decided to pay her first visit to the institute. She knew she wouldn't have time to really start anything, but in the original terminology of one of her favorite science fiction writers, she wanted to "grok" the building. As far as she could translate, the word meant "to absorb or view with absorption." And that was just what she needed. She would assess the exhibits, probably look at all of them. Then she would concentrate on the area of her main interest. In addition she would talk with the people who managed the exhibits and take a quick look at the institute's library.

She was just sliding into the bucket seat of her car,

having already put her purse onto the seat next to her, when a car pulled into the drive behind her.

For one startled moment she thought the arrival might by Ryder, and her heart started hammering accordingly. But by crinkling her eyes against the bright sunlight, Brianna could see that the car was a green sedan and that the man getting out had a head full of carrot-red hair. It was Paul.

"Do I come carrying a white flag? Or are you going to shoot first and ask questions later?" he asked warily.

Brianna eased herself from behind the wheel. She wanted to smile, but she didn't. She had prided herself that this morning she had been able to totally put from her mind all that had happened yesterday—a kind of forced amnesia. But with Paul's arrival it all came rushing back with sickening speed.

"That depends upon what you're going to say," she decided.

Paul grinned, his brown eyes deceivingly cheerful. "Could I have a cup of coffee? I always apologize best when I've got some false courage in my hand."

At that Brianna did let a little smile escape. "I thought it was liquor that gave false courage."

"I don't drink hard liquor, so it has to be coffee."

Brianna relented. "All right. Come on in."

Paul hesitated. "Are you going anywhere important? I can come back later."

Brianna leaned into her car to get her purse. "Nowhere I can't go another time."

Paul fell into step beside her. She led him into the kitchen.

"This may take a minute. I haven't completely familiarized myself with everything yet."

"The kettle's in the far left cabinet," he informed her.

Brianna turned to look at him.

"Try it," he urged.

When Brianna brought out a cherry-red enamel kettle, he commented smugly, "Doesn't everyone keep theirs in the far left cabinet?"

"You must have been here before for coffee."

"I told you I know the owner."

Brianna made no comment; instead she filled the kettle with water and placed it on a burner.

"Do you want to go into the living room?"

"No, let's stay in here. It's nice and cozy."

Wordlessly she took a chair beside the table and Paul followed suit.

Then he wasted no further time by coming directly to the point. "I came by to see you because I want to apologize."

"Oh?"

"Brianna"—his brown eyes became serious—"Anna and I didn't know about the article Ryder did until just before you came. She called me and told me about it while we were at my office."

Brianna remembered a call he had had that seemed to make a momentary dent in his friendly expression.

"What could we do?" he asked. "Ryder is a friend of ours, a good friend. Anna grew up in the house next to this one and—"

"What?"

Brianna had sat up straight as she thought she heard something out of place.

"I said Anna grew up living next door to Ryder and his family."

"But you said this one!"

Paul sighed. "I might as well tell you all of it, not keep anything back, then, after that, if you still don't want to have anything more to do with Anna and myself, we'll try to understand. I'll be up front with you. Okay?"

Brianna nodded, her green eyes wide.

"Ryder owns this house."

At Paul's quiet admission an electrified spark shot through Brianna's blood.

"Everything else I told you is true," Paul hurried on to say. "He doesn't live here anymore—hasn't for a long time—and he's thinking of selling."

"But why—"

"He said you needed a place. Brianna, Ryder isn't as bad as you think. He cares about people."

Brianna made a disbelieving noise.

"He really does. Do you know in that column he writes he's helped more people. He's made a number angry, but he's done a tremendous amount of good too. He's always trailing after some kind of injustice, trying to set it straight."

"He's beginning to sound like Superman," Brianna murmured dryly.

"In a way he is."

"Oh, come on, Paul! That's stupid. No one has super powers."

Paul laughed. "That's not exactly what I meant."

He sat forward, his forearms resting on the table, his fingers intertwined. "Ryder isn't afraid to step on toes."

"So I know."

Paul made a dismissing gesture. "He was having a little fun with you, that's all. What I'm talking about are big toes—politicians, unions, big business. Anna and I worry about him."

"He can take care of himself."

"So far, yes. But recently he had an 'accident' that was a near miss. He ended up more than a little bruised."

Brianna shrugged. She pretended that what Paul was saying was having no effect on her, but deep inside herself there was a stirring of some emotion she could not identify.

"So what does that have to do with me?" She continued to be offhand.

Paul narrowed his gaze and looked at her speculatively. When he could not pierce her cool, collected facade, he sighed, "Nothing, I suppose. I was just trying to explain."

"You said Anna lived near here?"

"The house next door, the one on the corner."

"Does her family still?"

"No. They moved several years ago."

She wanted to ask but held her tongue. However, Paul must have read her mind because he answered anyway.

"Ryder's are gone too. His parents were killed about eight years ago, and his sister died a year after that."

Again Brianna said nothing, and the whistling kettle gave her an excuse to move away from the table.

"I don't really want any of that," Paul said quietly.

"Neither do I," Brianna agreed.

She left the kettle on a back burner and came back to stand beside the table.

Paul got to his feet as well. "That's all I wanted to tell you. If you decide you don't want to continue staying here, I'll do what I can to help you find another place. And if you still want to think badly of Anna and me, well, I guess you couldn't be blamed. But will you at least think about what I've said?"

Brianna nodded. "I'll think about it."

"That's all anyone can ask," he replied, then reaching into his jacket pocket withdrew a leather pad and scribbled something on a piece of paper clasped within. "Here." He ripped the sheet off. "This is our telephone number. If you ever need us for anything..." He let the sentence trail into nothingness.

Brianna took it. "Thank you."

After Paul had gone Brianna experienced a new kind of restlessness. Somehow, knowing that this house belonged to Ryder made it seem less comfortable. Even the very air seemed to whisper of him. But she knew that it was all in her mind. The house was the same one she had fallen in love with. It couldn't help who held papers to it, who had lived here previously. So she couldn't blame it—just as she couldn't continue to blame Paul and Anna.

Of Ryder she was even more confused. She didn't

want to hear good things about him. He had told her practically from their first meeting that he was the "bad guy," and he had happily lived up to the role. Now to be told that he wasn't quite as unscrupulous as she had mentally painted him was something she was going to have to become adjusted to slowly. But that still didn't change the way he had acted toward her.

And if she were as honest with herself as Paul had been, she would concede that at the core of her anger was a deep hurt at the way Ryder had rejected her—cold-bloodedly, without feeling—at a time when she was anything but! And compared to that, everything else, including her father's job, came somewhere farther down the line. But it was hard for her to own up to; just as it was hard to remember. So, when the fleeting admission first raised its tiny head, Brianna crushed it down as if it were some kind of poisonous adder ready to strike at the elemental life force of her being. As a result, more confusion reigned.

Partly to keep her mind occupied, and partly to get away from the problems of this century, Brianna gratefully drove to the institute.

Finding the area where the institute was located was not all that difficult. Since it was a part of what had once been the site of a world's fair, all Brianna had to do was drive toward the tall, thin, needlelike monument that dominated the city's skyline.

The building that housed the history of the various ethnic groups who had lived in Texas from even before the dawn of recorded history was positioned in a far corner of the complex. It was very modern in appearance, with low sleek lines and a fountain of shooting water installed on one side of its front entrance while a contemporary cement waterfall was placed on the other.

Inside, a visitor could spend hours moving slowly from one exhibit to the next. Time was capsuled according to culture: Indian, French, Spanish, Mexican, German...The list went on and on, all the peoples who had left their mark on the state.

For Brianna it was like giving a child a free ice cream cone on a hot, sweltering day. She moved from one display case to the next, from one artifact to the other. She didn't concentrate on one period—she wanted to see it all!

She was standing for the second time before a glassed-in exhibit, examining a child's pair of Indian moccasins decorated with beautiful hand-worked beaded embroidery, when she slowly became aware that someone was standing across the case from her, watching with just as much intentness, but with their eyes directed at her rather than at what was residing within.

With startled realization Brianna met Ryder Cantrell's magnetic blue gaze, and for a moment, she couldn't pull her eyes away. A clamoring of emotions churned within her, as with no difficulty at all, she was catapulted back to those few blissful moments when he had been making love to her, before he had pulled away. The way he was looking at her now might have been a continuation, and Brianna's lips started to tingle and a warmth rose from deep within her to meet his warmth. The tip of her tongue came out to moisten the soft skin of her bottom lip, and she saw his eyes darken at that unconscious sensual act.

Then the arrival of a little girl, hurrying excitedly to get to the case, interrupted the concentration of their line of communication, and Brianna was able to drag her gaze away. From the corner of her eye she saw Ryder move, and she knew he was coming toward her.

Shaken, she wanted to hurry away. Never had she expected that one look could cause so much upheaval! But she couldn't run—she had nowhere to run to—and she didn't want to admit how much he had affected her, either to him or to herself. So, steeling her body for an exercise in protection, she turned as he came near and asked with a touch of pretended sarcasm, "Don't you have anything better to do than follow me?"

Ryder's blue eyes, still disturbingly dark, slowly examined her face. Then a small measure of his lazy smile appeared. "As a matter of fact, I do."

"Well then?" she demanded. "Why aren't you doing it?"

"I am."

"I don't understand." Brianna felt cast adrift on an inland sea.

"I came here to meet a man. He hasn't shown up yet, but you did."

"Oh." Ridiculously she felt disappointment. Not that she had wanted him to be looking for her—that was the absolutely last thing she would have wanted!

She decided she was still suffering from the upset she had experienced the moment before. She wasn't accustomed to so many emotional ups and downs. "So what will you do now?" she asked for something to say.

"Continue to wait."

"Does it concern your column?" She was remembering Paul's side of the conversation a few hours before.

"Yes."

She started to move forward, and Ryder came with her, his fingers hooked comfortably in the back pockets of his faded jeans. In a plaid shirt and dark brown boots that had seen better days, he looked for all the world as if he was a wrangler just come in off the range.

Brianna fingered the gold chain that circled her throat. She was unsure of what she should do next. He was walking with her and it seemed as if he had every intention of continuing to do so. Should she tell him she had to leave even though she wasn't ready yet? Or did she just calmly tell him that she didn't want him with her? And was that totally the truth? Damn, she wished she had spent more of her time the past ten years learning how to deal with situations like this with some form of self-possessed ease rather than writing about made-up ones. In fantasy, she could direct both sets of dialogue. In reality, she was incapable of doing either. Ryder continually said things she never expected him to, and she spent most of her time reacting!

They moved beside an old-fashioned buggy that came from the previous century. It was an open display and Ryder reached out to touch the metal rim of one wheel.

"I wonder if someday, a few hundred years from now, someone will look at a replica of my car in a museum and say, 'Can you believe they actually traveled in that?'" He smiled across at her.

Brianna ran a finger along a wooden spoke. "Probably. That's what I find so fascinating about history." She looked about her. "People actually used these things, touched them. Those people had faces, names, others who loved them; they had worries, sicknesses, fears, favorite songs; they enjoyed the same sun and moon that we do, smelled the same types of flowers, looked up to special leaders."

Ryder took her arm as they continued walking. "Do you wish you had been born in another time?"

"Is this on the record, or off?"

Ryder appreciated her very accurate dig. "Off."

Brianna answered then, "No, do you?"

He lifted a negligent shoulder. "Oh, sometimes. I think I'd make a pretty good Roman senator."

Brianna stopped walking for a moment, causing him to do so as well. "A Roman senator?"

"Sure. All the intrigue."

"And the possibility of sudden death."

He shrugged again. "That hasn't changed very much over the years."

Brianna started walking again, her forehead wrinkled. Was he really as blasé about danger as all that?

"At least people don't get away with poisoning each other today like they did then."

"No—"

"So?"

"I still think it would be an interesting time period."

To ease the troubling thoughts that had descended on her mind, Brianna decided to lighten the situation by saying, "Somehow I can't see you in a toga."

Laughing blue eyes met hers. "Somehow, neither can I. I guess I'll just be glad to stay right where I am."

They paused beside an exhibit that housed the contents of an old-time barbershop in the early nineteen hundreds: soap mugs, a leather strap for sharpening razors, an antique chair....

They examined it for a while, then Ryder seemed to become impatient. Brianna had noticed him taking occasional looks around the great room—she assumed for the person he was supposed to meet.

"Is he still not here?" she asked.

"No."

They started to move again, but before many steps Ryder stopped.

"I've had it with waiting. If he wants to see me again, he can call." But he still retained possession of her arm.

His gaze came back to look deeply into her own. "Are you almost through here for today?"

There was an inexplicable tightening to Brianna's breathing ability and a quickening of her blood. She had planned to stay on until the building closed at five, but suddenly now it wasn't all that important. She was going to be in San Antonio for a month to six weeks—what was one tiny portion of an afternoon?

"Just about." She was pleased with how casual her reply sounded.

"Then why don't we go out to dinner? Have you been on the River Walk yet?"

"No." Not for anything was she going to tell him she didn't even peek out her hotel window to see it.

"I think you'd like it. Why don't I pick you up about"—he checked his wristwatch—"five thirty? Okay?"

Brianna knew she was stupid for even considering it. Look what he had done to her before! But time was rapidly blunting the edge of what had happened as she again began to experience the same attraction she had felt before, that same magic.

"Er...yes. That would be fine."

"Do you like Mexican food?"

"I'm not sure. I don't think I've ever eaten any."

"Then you've got a treat coming. I'll make reservations for us at Casa del Rio."

"All right."

Ryder lightly squeezed her arm, his dark blue eyes warm, and then he walked away.

Brianna followed his lean figure until it disappeared behind a wall. She knew he didn't need to ask where she lived.

Brianna was ready by five fifteen. And that in itself was a miracle. As soon as she had realized what she had committed herself to, she had hurried out of the institute and did a quick walk-run to her car. It had been after four when he asked her to dinner, and she knew she was going to need a lot of time in order to get ready. The shower soap was still in its wrapper somewhere in one of the grocery bags she had meant to bring upstairs and had failed to do, her dress would need pressing. Brianna had sped into the house, sure that she would never be ready in time. But she was. And the minutes remaining hung heavily on her hands. More than once she walked over to the narrow gilded mirror in the hallway and checked her appearance. The soft yellow summer dress complemented her coloring perfectly, bringing out the blondness of her hair. She could have been a vision of gold except for the emerald green of her eyes. With some uneasiness she wondered if the bodice of the sundress was a little too low and tight. Other times she had not worried about it, but this time she wasn't sure.

The ringing of the doorbell halted her speculation. Nervously she ran suddenly damp palms along the material of her full skirt.

Ryder was waiting at the door. He was dressed in dark slacks and a dark shirt, which only emphasized the darkness of his skin. His rich brown hair was freshly combed although the curling texture rebelled against being too smoothly held. His eyes ran over her in one quick assessing motion. Then he spoke.

"May I come in?"

Brianna stupidly had forgotten to say anything and

she was disgusted with herself. She was a grown woman! She shouldn't be acting as if she were totally inexperienced. She had been out many times before with men who were interesting. But not with any quite so aggressively attractive to her, the little voice deep inside her maintained. She made herself move out of the way.

"Of course. It is your home."

Ryder came across the threshold. "No," he disagreed. "It's yours...for as long as the lease states. I'm just a visitor."

But even as he said that, he turned his head so that he could see all of the hall and the two rooms on either side. It was as if he was remembering.

"Would you like to sit down, have a drink?" Brianna asked a little nervously. She had never before entertained someone in their own house and didn't quite know how to go about it. Because even though he had said the place was hers, she didn't feel that it was. "I'm limited to instant coffee or Coke, but if you wouldn't mind that..."

Ryder's gaze came back to her. "I don't need anything."

Brianna moved restlessly, feeling the imprint of his eyes. She could sense them going over her again, only this time with more leisure and appreciation.

"You could be a golden butterfly," he murmured softly, "all gossamer wings and delicate body."

Once more Brianna was startled by his words. She had not expected that he could be so poetic. He didn't seem the sort.

"Er . . . thank you." She knew she was blushing but couldn't help herself. "You—you look nice yourself."

There! The romance writer, who should have been the one spouting beautifully formed words, sounded more like the tongue-tied, tough reporter.

His smile told her that possibly he was thinking along those exact lines. "Thanks, this was just something I threw on."

His use of the old feminine cliché reinforced her suspicion.

Typically, Brianna decided to call his bluff. Yet she said it with a disarming smile; she didn't want to be the one to create another hostile strain between them before they had even begun the evening. "Are you making fun of me?"

"No, not really."

"For a minute I thought you were."

He took a step toward her and reached out to grasp her arm in a light hold. "I think we'd better leave, otherwise we might never make it to our dinner."

The sensation set up by the touch of his fingers on her bare skin was enough to melt Brianna into a pool of quivering womanhood. She knew she was being stupid, knew she was laying the groundwork for the possibility of more hurt, but she could do nothing to resist. Just as she couldn't seem to keep her mind from jumping ahead to a speculation as to what they would do if they didn't leave the house. A delicious quiver of remembrance slowly floated up her spine. It was only the following memory of his withdrawal that warned her not to rush headlong into something neither of them might be prepared to deal with at that moment.

Gathering herself, she asked, "Did you have any trouble getting reservations?"

"No, the manager's a friend of mine."

"So you do have friends."

"A few."

"But more enemies?"

He lifted a casual shoulder.

"Doesn't that bother you?"

His thumb began a languid circular movement on the inner flesh of her arm just above her elbow. "Only if you still think of yourself as one. Have you forgiven me?"

At one time—had it only been yesterday?—she would have given him an emphatic *no*! But now, just a spare twenty-four hours later, she wasn't so sure. She had never thought she could have accepted what he had done so quickly, but, looking within herself, acknowledging the way her body was responding to his caress, she could find no stain of rancor left.

From the very beginning, from the time she had looked up at the bookstore and found him watching her, she had been drawn to him—even to the point of instantly wanting to be the recipient of his lovemaking. And she had been an active participant in the later near granting of that wish.

Now she was wanting him again. Yet this time she wanted to get closer to him in more than a physical way. She wanted to get into his brain, learn more of the way he thought, see if what Paul had said about him was true.

"I'm trying to," she whispered, incapable of making her voice stronger.

The stroking on her arm ceased, but still he retained possession. "At least that's a start."

Brianna's spirit sang with a tentative sort of joy as she sat beside Ryder in the low bucket seat of his sports car. There had been no exchange of words since they had become enclosed in the fiberglass and metal cocoon, but somehow there wasn't the need for any.

As they approached the area of the hotel where Brianna spent her first nights in San Antonio, Ryder broke the silence.

"I hope you're not starving. I didn't make the reservations until nine."

"Nine?"

"I've got something special planned."

"Oh?"

"It's a surprise."

"Won't you give me a hint?"

"No. Can you wait?"

Since Brianna's stomach had never felt less like accepting food, she easily could agree.

"We can get a snack, if you like, to tide us over," he suggested.

"Are you hungry?" She remembered his liking for food when they were in Dallas.

"A little."

"Do *you* want a snack?"

"I wouldn't mind some nachos."

"What's that?"

Ryder looked across at her in humorous disbelief. "You really don't know?"

She shook her head.

He smiled. "Lord, have you got an education coming to you. And I'll gladly be your teacher."

Words sprang to her mouth, but she instantly censored them. Things were going too smoothly. She was not going to rock the boat. Maybe he didn't like aggressive women. Maybe that had been part of the problem in Dallas. And heaven knew, being aggressive in a sexual way had never been her way of behaving. It had only happened with him.

"Should I call you Mr. Cantrell, then?"

"You do and I won't let you have any nachos."

"Then I won't."

"Good decision."

If Brianna had wondered how they were going to spend the three hours between the time they arrived and the time their dinner reservations were set for, she was not left in doubt for long.

Ryder parked the car and ushered her into a walkway between two buildings. They then found themselves at the top of some grass-lined steps that were spotted with people sitting in an open-air amphitheater listening to the sounds of a mariachi band whose members were standing on a low-set stage across a narrow waterway.

Brianna's first impression was of the beauty of the scene before her, both visual and auditory. The brass horns, the guitars, the white stuccoed building positioned behind the stage proudly displaying Spanish arches, the profusion of greenery. She turned a wide, appreciative gaze to Ryder. His eyes crinkled in return.

For a time they listened, then, with his hand to the small of her back, they descended the stairs and started along a walkway that followed the trail of the jade-green water.

A beautiful arch built of white limestone soon appeared and served to connect one side of land to the other. Some people were standing at the apex, leaning against the ridge, looking across at the panorama she and Ryder were just leaving.

Brianna didn't have to be told that this must be the famed River Walk, the Paseo del Rio. And before they had gone much farther she could understand why it was the number-one tourist spot in San Antonio, and why he had told her to be sure to see it. It was cool, cypress trees lining the water and giving shade; green, a mass of growing things carefully landscaped along its lowered banks—ferns, ivy, grasses—and there was an atmosphere of relaxation, a graceful peace, that could never be found in other inner cities.

Couples strolled beside the river, along the narrow paths that were bordered by low rock walls and occasional man-made waterfalls, following the water as it wound its way through the center of town. Flat, motor-driven barges loaded with people toured from one end of the twisting waterway to the other. Restaurants of varying kinds and expense vied for visitors' custom. And still, an occasional arch stretched itself across the water, used for decorative beauty as well as functional need.

Nachos, Brianna discovered, were crunchy bits of fried corn tortillas that had been covered with melted cheese and slices of green jalapeño pepper. And they were delicious. In the end she ate as many as Ryder— only she left the peppers to him after having tried one and almost burned the tip of her tongue off. His eyes twinkling devilishly, Ryder only laughed and popped another into his mouth.

As the sun began to set, artificial lighting was switched on, and the area started to take on an entirely different quality. And when darkness totally fell, Brianna didn't remember ever having been in a more romantic place. The water reflected the multiple, yet subtly placed lights, couples seemed to walk a little slower and more closely, conversation became more intimate, the sound of music seemed to drift more lightly on the gentle breeze.

Yet all the while they had been walking, Ryder had done no more than touch her back occasionally, in the main to direct the direction of her footsteps. And even now he did no more.

Brianna began to feel more than a little bereft. She knew she was being silly but that didn't stop her from feeling that way. She wasn't repulsive! And she knew for a fact that she didn't leave him cold, so why was he acting this way? Couldn't he at least hold her hand? Or put an arm around her shoulders as he once had? Was he afraid that she might attack if he did? Good God! Just what did he think she was?

When they arrived at the restaurant, Brianna found that they had passed it earlier in the evening. Round umbrella-covered tables were placed along the sidewalk and were broken only by a small path that allowed strollers the right to pass by. Waiters busily moved from table to table and people were enjoying a variety of deliciously smelling foods. There were only a few tables left, and Brianna wondered which would be theirs. She hoped they might get one at the edge of the water.

"Ryder!" A man calling his name from behind them brought both of their heads about.

"James." Ryder swung about to extend his hand to the person who came rushing up. He was tall and dark with the dark, flashing eyes of his Mexican ancestry, and his round face was a mirror of his pleasure.

"I'm so happy to see you, my friend." His words were slightly accented. "It's been too long since you've last been here."

Ryder released his hand. "That it has. And I haven't eaten any good Mexican food in all that time, either."

"You'd better not. If you had, I'd be upset."

"And we couldn't have that."

"No, definitely not." Eyes of the darkest brown roamed over Brianna with evident interest, taking in the classical lines of her face, the fall of honey-blond hair, and the shapeliness of her figure in the yellow

Enter a uniquely American world of romance with

Harlequin American Romance.™

Harlequin American Romances are the first romances to explore today's new love relationships. These compelling romance novels reach into the hearts and minds of women across America...probing into the most intimate moments of romance, love and desire.

You'll follow romantic heroines and irresistible men as they boldy face confusing choices. Career first, love later? Love without marriage? Long-distance relationships? All the experiences that make love real are captured in the tender, loving pages of *Harlequin American Romance*.

What makes American women so different when it comes to love? Find out with *Harlequin American Romance!* Send for your introductory FREE book now.

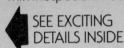

dress. "Are you going to introduce me," he said at last, "or do I have to introduce myself?"

Ryder laughed softly and in a pretended aside warned, "Watch him, Brianna. He likes blondes."

"What man in his right mind would not?"

"And redheads, and brunettes...."

All right, all right!" He held up his hands in mock surrender. "I concede."

"Just so she gets the idea."

James raised himself to his full height, which was several inches above Ryder and demanded imperiously, "Are you going to introduce me?"

Copying his friend's stance of dignity, Ryder nodded and said, "Brianna St. Clair meet James Diego Ramirez, the manager of Casa del Rio. James, meet Brianna."

"I am honored," James replied, then, breaking into a white-toothed grin, bent low over Brianna's hand and kissed it.

Deciding to take part in the charade the two men were playing, Brianna swept into a low, deep curtsy, and replied, "The honor is mine, senor." She met his dark gaze and broke into a conspiratorial grin.

"Ahh, Ryder." James turned to her companion beaming. "This time you have found the right one! I, James Diego Ramirez, say that I am pleased!"

He squeezed Brianna's hand then gave it to an unprotesting Ryder. Ryder took it but didn't comment on his friend's statement.

Instead he asked, "Is everything ready?"

Mysteriously, at least to Brianna, James replied,

"All gassed up and waiting. Take as long as you like. For my friends, I will do anything."

"Now I suppose you'd like a medal," Ryder murmured dryly.

"Just a little one," James agreed.

"A little gold one."

"Or a little silver."

"You shouldn't be greedy."

"Why not? Everyone else is."

"James, you know you're not everyone else."

The manager sighed. "That is true. Then I'll just take a thank you."

"You've got it."

"Enjoy, my friend," James wished and turning to Brianna, "You too, my new friend. And take care of this one, okay? No one else does."

"Hurry up, Brianna," Ryder urged, pulling her forward, "before he starts to tell you the story of my life."

Of necessity Brianna went with him, but she glanced around just before they turned to weave in and out of the assembled tables. She was in time to see that James's smile had disappeared and in its place was something that could only be read as concern. Her heart gave a funny little plunge.

Chapter Six

The surprise Brianna had been promised was indeed that. Because instead of leading her to a table, Ryder took her to the edge of the water and motioned for her to step aboard one of the docked barges that traveled the river. For a moment, Brianna hesitated. What were they going to do on a barge? Then her eyes widened as she took in the presence of a small table covered with a white cloth, a grouping of lavender and white chrysanthemums in a glass vase, a table setting, a smiling waiter, and a boy who was to guide the expedition.

"Do you like it?" Ryder asked.

"It's wonderful!" Brianna returned, stepping aboard. Ryder came with her, still holding her hand. He saw her to her seat, took his, and then nodded at the helmsman. The boat's motor started up, and they slowly inched away from the side.

Brianna gazed appreciatively at their surroundings, her eyes shining with tiny images of the restaurant's gold-colored lights strung above them. Her hands were now both resting in her lap, but she could still feel the impression of his fingers.

"Wine, senor?" The waiter's question intruded upon her dreamy state.

"Please."

Excitement stirred as Brianna watched Ryder taste the small portion of wine the waiter poured and then nodded his approval. His eyes met hers as their glasses were filled.

"I thought this might appeal to you." The breeze, increased by the boat's gentle passage, ruffled some springy tufts of his hair, causing them to fall forward over his forehead.

Brianna controlled her desire to reach out and push them back by reaching instead for her wineglass. She took a sip of the light, smooth liquid. "It's very romantic."

"Appropriate, especially for you."

She knew he was referring to her occupation and not the state of her emotions, so she agreed by inclining her head.

"I ordered our meal when I made the reservation. I hope you like it."

"I'm sure I will," Brianna assured him softly.

Ryder said nothing; he just continued to look at her, his eyes seemingly as mysterious as the night surrounding them.

An hour later, the barge redocked. The meal had been delicious and Brianna was converted to the new passion of loving Mexican food. Guacamole, enchaladas, tacos, chili, refried beans—each was a revelation in taste and seasoning. And the conversation had been satisfactory as well. They had talked of many things, none of them of earth-shaking importance, and yet she had learned something of Ryder. She now knew he was a basketball fan—especially of the Spurs, the San Antonio team; he belonged to a car club in the city, where each of the members owned a Corvette, and that he had come in second in the last rally they had held; that he hated onions; he loved the University of Texas where he had gone to college; and his favorite fiction writer was Robert Ludlum.

And something else seemed to have happened during the sixty minutes they enjoyed their open-air, floating dinner. She could sense that maybe, just maybe, Ryder had come to regard her a little differently. She couldn't say exactly how, or what had caused it, but when they exited the restaurant, by mutual agreement they didn't turn back toward where the car was parked. They again walked beside the river, only this time they were the ones walking slowly, with his arm draped warmly across her shoulders, the periodic word they exchanged about the beauty of the area, low and intimate.

As they drove back to the house, Brianna leaned her head against the high seat back and smiled gently to herself. It had been a marvelous evening, nearly as close to perfection as she had ever spent before. And she knew that most of the reason could be applied to only one person: Ryder.

She turned her head so that she could look at him. He was sitting comfortably behind the wheel, driving smoothly and competently, his eyes on the road. Her gaze traveled over him and she felt a rush of emotion.

She didn't understand what it was she felt, but it was there. And it wasn't entirely a physical need. Oh, that was there too—his lean hard body called out to her, his strong profile emphasizing his appeal. But it was something more.

The trip didn't last long. Where she lived was not that far away from the central portion of town. In fact, Ryder confided, the same river they had been walking along ran just a few blocks from his house.

When the car pulled into the driveway and Ryder cut the engine, Brianna suddenly became a bundle of indecision. She wanted to ask him in, but how would he take it? She didn't want to do anything at the last moment that would ruin the evening they had spent.

Ryder took the necessity of making a choice away from her by coming around to her side of the car and opening the door. He smiled when she stood up, and motioned for her to precede him.

Brianna walked along the side of the house beside the arched porchway. She went up the two steps that led to the front door. But this time the steadiness of her fingers wasn't as accurate as the time before when he had been coming inside her hotel room. This time her fingers were trembling, and he had to take the keys from her in order to let them in.

Once inside Brianna hurriedly asked if he would like some coffee. When he agreed, she walked quickly into the kitchen, where she had to take a minute to regain her breath. But Ryder didn't leave her alone for long. He too came into the room.

"I haven't been back here for years. Do you mind if I watch while you make the coffee?"

"Er...no. Not at all." Now if that wasn't a bald-faced lie, she had never seen one! She did mind! She wanted him in the other room so that she could finish collecting herself; but, glancing at him, he didn't look as if he was about to budge from his leaning position against the heavy wooden table, and she didn't think she would be able to bodily toss him out. So she made the best of the situation and willed her nerves to come to order. Then, as an excuse to give him something to think about rather than concentrating solely upon what she was doing, she asked, "You said you haven't been here in a long time?"

Ryder frowned. "No."

"Paul told me your parents had died."

Ryder shifted his position.

"I'm sorry," she commiserated.

He shrugged. "It can't be helped."

"How did it happen?"

"A freeway accident. They were coming home from taking my sister to the university in Austin. Their car was rear ended and burst into flame."

Brianna halted in the act of switching on the burner. "That's terrible!"

He grimaced. "It wasn't very easy at the time."

"Did you have to tell your sister?"

"Yes."

"That must have been hard."

"It was."

Brianna paused. She hesitated to add to his sadness,

but it was already there; she could see it in the tightness of his mouth. "And your sister died the next year?"

"Yes."

Ryder folded his arms across his chest and lowered his head. Brianna felt an immediate aching, as if she were somehow sharing his memory.

"She must not have been very old."

"Nineteen."

"How—how did she die?"

When he remained silent, Brianna turned back to the stove and further adjusted the switch to the burner under the kettle. She was being too nosy. They had learned something about each other this evening, but they weren't yet close enough to share deeper sentiments.

"Forget it. I shouldn't have asked," she apologized and reached into an upper cabinet for cups and saucers.

"She died from an abortion...a botched abortion."

Brianna's hand froze, and the cup she was in the act of lifting from the shelf dropped from her hand, splintering into a hundred pieces on the ceramic counter top and covering, as well, a portion of the floor.

So that was it! That was why he had put the part in his article about unwed mothers and abortion clinics... why he had intimated that she and others like her were in some way to be blamed. But did he really feel that way? She didn't see how he possibly could. He was an educated man, an intelligent man. He could see that one fact did not automatically follow the other.

The table legs scraped as Ryder jerked forward, trying to keep her from stepping back on a piece of cup remnant.

But Brianna was not about to move. She couldn't. And when Ryder's arms came out to enfold her, she could only look up at him with wide horrified eyes set in a face that had become chalk-white.

"Oh, God, Ryder. I'm sorry," she whispered huskily. She wished she had never asked, wished she had never brought up any of it. She would have been better off not knowing.

Ryder's tanned face was close, and for a time he too seemed to forget about moving. His expression tightened even more as he continued to look at her.

Finally he spoke, "No, you're not the one who should apologize. I should. I gave you a pretty cheap shot in that article, and I knew better. But some devil seemed to take hold of me and the next thing I knew I was calling in the story."

Brianna continued to stare at him. He was apologizing!

Carefully Ryder pulled her away from the scene of the breakage.

"Did you cut yourself?" he asked, his eyes running over her hands and arms.

"No, I don't think so," Brianna answered a little blankly, still stunned by all that had happened.

"That cup sounded like a bomb going off."

It was funny, but Brianna remembered no sound other than the echo of his words.

"Yes."

Ryder gave an impatient sigh. "You should go wash off. There may be slivers of glass on your skin."

Brianna blinked and nodded her head in agreement, but instead of moving, she continued to watch as Ryder walked toward a slender side closet in the corner of the room and withdrew a broom. Fascinated, she saw that he was serious about cleaning up the mess.

When he was almost done with the floor, Brianna gave a small start and realized she had yet to do as he suggested. On legs that were still a bit unsteady she moved to the sink, turned on the water, and found that he was correct—there were little particles of the broken cup adhering to the fine golden hairs of her lower arm. After washing them off, she used the cloth to brush the bodice of her dress.

When she turned, it was to find that she was the object of Ryder's observation.

"Why don't you go into the living room and sit down. I'll make the coffee," he offered quietly.

Brianna started to protest but decided against it. Maybe he needed the moment to be alone just as she did. With a short assenting dip of her head she moved to the doorway that led into the hall.

When Ryder came into the room carrying a tray and two cups of steaming coffee, Brianna sat forward onto the edge of the overstuffed couch. Ryder placed the tray on the low table before her and then took a seat at her side.

Brianna stirred in her usual spoonful of sugar and raised the cup to her lips. The coffee was strong but it tasted good, and the very briskness of it helped her to regain a little of her normal stability.

"I'm sorry I made you remember all of that, Ryder." She held the cup's handle tightly.

"You didn't make me do anything," he disagreed.

"You didn't have to apologize." Her green eyes lifted to his.

He hesitated for only a second before replying, "I think I did. I pride myself on trying to be fair in my reporting. I wasn't to you. So—" He shrugged lightly, letting the rest of the sentence finish itself. "But I didn't expect it to have that much effect."

Brianna looked away. In truth, she still had not completely recovered from his revelation, but at least that knowledge helped her to understand the reasoning behind the seeming unfeeling action a little better now. "It was just the shock," she murmured.

Ryder moved to place his cup on the low table before reaching out to bring her face around, one long finger at her chin.

"I apologize for that too," he said softly.

Brianna's gaze was held by his, and a warm glow began to grow in the pit of her stomach in spite of the previous seriousness of their talk.

"Did I totally destroy the evening?" he asked, his half smile pulling with less sureness than usual. It was as if he too no longer wanted to dwell on the past and regretted the loss of enchantment that had earlier surrounded them.

"No," Brianna husked.

His smile increased and the look of strain was removed. Then from the message that gradually began to build in his eyes Brianna knew he was going to kiss her.

"Good, because I didn't mean to." He was leaning closer.

"No."

The repetition of her previous answer was not heeded by either of them. And it certainly wasn't meant as a denial of what was about to happen.

Brianna's mouth parted as Ryder's lips first came into gentle contact with her own. But for breathtaking seconds, as they continued to drift, lightly suspended, teasing her sensitive skin, Brianna's excitement heightened until she didn't think she was going to be able to stand it.

And when finally the excruciating misery of his nearness had rekindled all her bursting need of him, his mouth came down completely, and she responded to the demanding flare of passion within her by lifting her arms about his neck and pulling herself closer, molding her body to his.

She could feel the warmth of his skin through his shirt, feel the quickening tenor of his breathing, touch the hard muscles of his shoulders and chest.

It was a kiss like none she had ever received before...except once, at the hotel. And Brianna wanted more, just as she had done then. But memory served her well. Before, when she had let things go so far, he had pulled away. This time, she couldn't afford to let that happen again. This time it must be she who called a halt.

But she couldn't do it just yet—no, not yet! His hands were moving over her back, along her ribs, caressing her heated skin through the thin material of her dress. His lips were moving on hers, seemingly trying to search for her very soul.

When she felt the first thrust of his tongue into the warm moistness of her mouth, Brianna gave a little jolt of surprise, of increased pleasure. But it was also because she knew that the time to pull away had to be now. Otherwise she wouldn't be able to control things for much longer.

It was one of the hardest things she had ever had to do in her life, but she did it. She broke the seal of their kiss and pushed herself back.

Ryder let her go, yet he still retained a loose possession of her shoulders. His eyes were a deep, dark blue as he looked at her.

"I like kissing you, Brianna," he whispered huskily. "I like holding you... touching you...."

Brianna said nothing. She couldn't. Her throat was too tight with longing.

Ryder sighed deeply, and his hands momentarily tightened their hold. Then they relaxed and he let them fall away.

"I think I'd better go. Before I overstay my welcome." He lifted his weight from the couch.

Again Brianna said nothing. She wanted to cry out for him to stay. But instinctively she knew that that was the wrong thing to do at this moment. There was a subtle difference in him this time—he wasn't out to prove anything. She might have her fleeting moment of satisfaction, but what about later? Would he come to her again? And would she want him to?

As these thoughts were running through her mind, Ryder walked to the door. Quickly Brianna shook herself free from her mental prison and hurried to catch up with him. She didn't want him to think she was angry with him in any way. She knew that thought was stupid, juvenile, but it was there. And she didn't want to take a chance.

"I enjoyed dinner, Ryder, and the River Walk." To her own ears, her voice sounded unnaturally high and unsure. But to her relief, Ryder seemed not to notice anything unusual.

"So did I."

He opened the door and started to walk through. For something to do Brianna put her hands on both the inner and outer sets of knobs and leaned her cheek against the wooden edge. Again, when she needed it most, dialogue would not pop into her mind. She was a muted heroine, pleading for the services of an excellent ghost-writer.

Ryder paused and looked back at her. Then his fingers came out to touch her exposed cheek. The tender salute made Brianna's eyes flutter shut as she dealt with the stirrings within herself.

"Take care of yourself, Brianna," he said easily. Then he was gone. And she was left breathless.

That night Brianna found sleep hard to attain. Her emotions were literally tied in knots. She didn't know how to take the man, what to do about him. And she wondered if she would ever have opportunity to debate the question again. He had said nothing about calling her. And, liberated as she was, she could not see herself calling him. After what had transpired between them in the beginning, she couldn't. She would have to wait. And that was the worst part.

She hated waiting! But she had learned to live with it because of her profession. Sometimes it seemed that half her life was spent waiting—particularly when she was just starting out. Waiting to see whether a publishing house liked her material, waiting to get word from her editor on the revisions she would have to make, waiting for galleys, waiting for the publication date, waiting for reader reaction, waiting for royalties.... Wait! Wait! Wait!

Brianna turned restlessly in the bed. Maybe she had done the wrong thing. Maybe she should have taken what might have come and been happy with it. She shouldn't have thought of the long run, because there might not be one.

Then again, how would she have felt about herself if she had encouraged him to stay? She had waited this long. What was a little longer? Few people would believe that she was a virgin. At her age? And when she wrote such steamy love scenes? They would laugh and tell her to pull the other one. But she was. And she had chosen to be. Until now she had found no man she wanted to give herself to that badly. And, to her mind, there was no substance to the trap of gaining experience just for the sake of having got it. Her answer to the radio talk-show host had been more

honest than even he had thought—she, herself, had
garnered a great deal of her knowledge of the more
intimate physical pleasures through reading and ab-
sorbing.

Only, now, ironically, when she had found the man
she wanted, she wasn't at all sure just how much he
wanted her. He certainly hadn't insisted. Not at all.
And he had been distant, to a degree, at the beginning
of the evening, only relaxing toward the end.

But maybe she was rushing things. Lord, they had
known each other for less than a week! Not exactly an
extended expanse of time.

Yes, possibly that was the answer. She needed to
give both of them more time.

Brianna turned on her side once again, reached out
for the pillow that was a twin to the one her head was
resting on, and hugged it to her breast. It was cool
where she was warm, and it gave her something to
hold on to. She couldn't help it if, just before she finally drifted into sleep, her unconscious mind transferred it into the warm, hard body of the man who
had been occupying her thoughts for so long.

For the next week Brianna worked very hard. She
spent her days at the institute library going through
researchers' notes, clippings, and memoirs, and her
nights reading what most Texas school children probably try to avoid—the dry textbook histories of their
state. To get a good picture of the period she was interested in, Brianna had to go both backward and
forward in time. She would never use a lot of the in-

formation she collected, but it was all part and parcel of knowing what she was doing.

Of Ryder, she heard nothing. Oh, she read his column—that was the first thing she turned to in the newspaper each day. She appreciated his style and the way he used humor to make a stinging point. And she could see where his fearlessness in challenging wrongs could, in some instances, cause him problems. His last article had been the impropriety of a large corporation in trying to "persuade" an old man to move out of his home so that they could expand their building when the man was determined not to go. In all likelihood, Ryder had the old man's eternal gratitude, but the executives of the business, a huge concern that specialized in the mass marketing of frozen Mexican foods, probably would like to lynch him.

As the weekend approached, Brianna decided to take a day off. After all, other people didn't drive themselves constantly, and just because she was a cruel taskmaster to herself didn't mean that she couldn't rebel and do what she wanted once in a while. She was just trying to decide what it was she was going to do when the telephone by her side began to ring.

An almost hurtful pang shot through her. Would that be Ryder? Her telephone didn't ring often, thank goodness—if it did, she would be nothing but a jumble of wrecked nerves by now.

She took a deep breath to steady her voice before answering, "Hello." She strove to get just the right amount of friendliness yet aloofness in her tone.

"Brianna? This is Anna. How are you?"

Brianna forced the disappointment she felt to the back of her mind. She had completely forgotten about Anna and Paul! She should have called them; they probably still thought she was upset.

"Anna! I'm fine. How are you?"

At her show of pleasure, Anna hesitated. Then she replied dryly, "Wondering if I should call, for one thing."

"Oh, well, yes. I should have called you before this myself."

"I wasn't sure— Paul said he had filled you in on all the gory details, but—"

Brianna interrupted, "Yes, he did."

"He said you said you'd think about it."

"Yes."

"And have you?"

Brianna lied a little. "Yes, but I didn't have to think for very long. I'm sorry I acted so stupidly. It wasn't your fault."

"Well, we think we're the ones who should be sorry. But for the heck of us we can't decide why. We won't apologize because Ryder is our friend. And we can't say that we knew what had happened and were trying to deceive you, because we didn't know anything about it until it was too late. So, there we are. What do we have to feel guilty for?"

"My sentiments exactly," Brianna agreed, smiling at the teasingly annoyed quality of the other woman's voice.

"So why don't you come over tomorrow afternoon and have a late lunch with us?"

"I'd love to." Instantly Brianna replaced her partially formulated plans for Saturday that had never really appealed very much anyway with this much more enjoyable proposition. "What time? And can I bring anything?"

"We thought we'd barbecue some burgers and maybe make some homemade ice cream."

"Sounds great."

"We'll eat around three. But come any time you want. And as for bringing anything—just bring yourself."

"All right, this time I will," Brianna agreed. "But soon, very soon, I want to do something nice for you and Paul. You're the first real friends I've made here."

A second passed before Anna replied, her inflection more serious than before, "I'm glad you feel that way. I hated it when you went away like that. I—I felt all ugly inside."

Brianna experienced a prick of conscience. Ryder had warned her to be careful. "You could never be that," she reassured, hoping belatedly to make up for her previous behavior.

"Thank you."

"I'll see you tomorrow afternoon then."

"We'll be looking forward to it."

As Brianna replaced the receiver she nibbled unconsciously on her bottom lip. At least some people realized that she was still alive.

Brianna slept late the following morning. As had been happening since the night she and Ryder had gone to dinner, she had been having trouble sleeping well. Her slumber was fitful...she would wake up at odd times and be unable to return to her unconscious state. Then all kinds of thoughts would jump into her head. She wondered just how serious the danger was to Ryder from his work. She remembered Paul's fears and the manager of the restaurant's worried look. Also she remembered his own admission of liking intrigue. And a puzzling knot would form in the region of her stomach. Next she would speculate about his previous marriage. He had told her it hadn't worked out. God, she hoped he had not lived with his wife in this house! That thought was definitely not appealing. Then she wondered about his wife, about what she had been like, about what had happened to cause the breakup of their marriage. And she wondered if he still loved her.

It was well after ten before she was up and had showered and was dressed, ready to do a few errands before going over to Paul's. One of the things she did was stop by a florist to collect an armful of beautiful cut flowers. Anna had said to bring nothing, but she was uncomfortable at the thought. After today they would have fed her twice, so she wanted to do something immediate to show her appreciation.

When she turned her car onto the street where they lived it was a little before one. She realized she was a trifle early, but Anna had said to come when she wanted.

The first thing Brianna noted upon coming to a stop before the house was the sleek black Corvette parked in the drive. There was a time when she would have experienced a black rage on seeing it, but this time her soul burst into a joyful little song.

He hadn't called, he hadn't come by, he hadn't seemed to care if she was alive or dead, but she still wanted to see him. And now it looked as if she was going to be granted that wish.

Collecting the bouquet from the seat next to her, Brianna shut the door of her Le Sabre and walked gracefully up the sidewalk to the front door. Her heart was pounding and her eyes were a clearer shade of green. She was glad she had worn her hair loose instead of in the braid she had contemplated wearing. And she was glad she had decided on shorts for the cookout—the bit of red material fitting smoothly over her trim hips and derriere, showing off the shapeliness of her legs—instead of a more conservative skirt or slacks. Her white blouse was trimmed with red piping and she knew she looked her best, even if casual.

Anna's face was worried when she answered the door.

"Brianna, Ryder's here. I couldn't get rid of him."

Brianna tried to keep her smile from seeming too glad.

"It's all right, Anna. I don't mind."

"You don't?" Her huge black eyes widened.

"No. Here." She thrust the flowers forward. "These are for you."

Anna took them and in a bit of a daze, backed away from blocking the door to let Brianna inside.

Once she was in the living room Brianna couldn't help the quick glance about she gave.

"The men are outside," Anna said flatly. Then, "I wish someone would give me a scorecard! I never know what's going on anymore!"

"Would you like me to put those in water for you?" Brianna asked in order to get Anna's mind onto something else.

"There's a vase on top of the refrigerator," she answered automatically.

"Good. I'll be right back."

Brianna swept the bouquet from Anna's hands and went into the kitchen. As she was filling the vase with water, she had a perfect view of the backyard. A twist of both apprehension and excitement strengthened as she saw Ryder's lean form standing in front of the opened garage next to Paul. They seemed to be discussing Paul's car. And the next thing that happened confirmed this. Ryder bent down on one knee to lower his field of vision until he was looking beneath the back of the car. With one hand on the rear bumper, he reached out to touch something that he saw. Then, after a moment, he stood back up and wiped his fingers on a handkerchief that he had pulled from his back pocket. Today, once again, he was dressed in jeans, only this time they were rust colored, and a cream pullover shirt that had wide stripes of rust, gold, and blue around its midsection.

"Did you find it?" Anna asked from behind her.

Brianna started then realized that the vase was overflowing with water and had been for some time.

Quickly she shut off the flow and tipped the excess out of the container.

"Ah, yes. I was just about done."

"Uh-huh, sure you were."

Brianna turned to see that Anna's eyes were alive with amusement.

"Do you always run the water for five minutes—just to be sure that you have the very best?" she asked.

A maddening hint of pink entered Brianna's cheeks. But she braved the moment out by retorting, "I think I read somewhere that water should be the freshest possible for flowers to last their longest."

Very tongue-in-cheek Anna replied, "It must have been in *Good Housekeeping*."

"I suppose." Brianna arranged the flowers.

"It wouldn't have anything to do with Ryder being out there."

Brianna pretended dissatisfaction with the position of a carnation.

Anna went on, "Because I've seen him have that kind of effect on women before."

That brought Brianna's gaze around. "You have?"

"Sure."

But she was unable to enlighten Brianna further because of the arrival of the men.

Paul was first into the kitchen. His brown eyes began to sparkle as he took in Brianna's presence.

"Hey! Look who's here! Good to see you, Brianna!'' He came across the room and gave her a brotherly hug. "Glad you could come."

Ryder halted in the doorway. Brianna saw the surprise register on his face as she looked at him over Paul's shoulder.

When Paul turned her loose she attached a warm smile to her lips.

"I'm glad I could come too. Hello, Ryder. I didn't expect to see you here." She supposed her motive in saying that was to let him know immediately that she wasn't trying to follow him.

His blue eyes traveled over her and she had to work hard to conceal the heated excitement that rose up to flood her senses. His slow smile emerged and he drawled easily, "I didn't expect to see you either." He shifted his gaze to Anna. "Now I understand your gentle hints to leave."

Anna had the grace to blush. "Well, I didn't know things had changed between you two," she complained. "The last time I saw you, Brianna wanted to slit your throat and you looked as if you'd like to choke her!"

Paul chuckled and murmured under his breath, "Uneven is the path of true love." Then he began to cough as Anna's elbow jabbed sharply in his ribs.

Brianna too had heard what he said but pretended not to. Whether Ryder did or not she couldn't tell. She hoped not. The idea of love had never entered her mind. She was fascinated by Ryder, was drawn to him, but she didn't feel love.

"Then since everything's out in the open and you

two are friends—Ryder, why don't you stay for lunch with us? We're having burgers courtesy of Paul,'' Anna prompted.

Paul took a mock bow. ''What she means is I'm going to burn some on the barbecue pit.''

Ryder came further into the room. Brianna's eyes couldn't seem to pull away from him, appreciating the easy way he moved, the way his clothing fit his body.

''When's all this going to happen?''

''Not for a couple of hours,'' Paul answered, checking his watch. ''Unless you're starving, Brianna.''

Brianna tore her gaze away from Ryder. ''Me? No...no, I'm fine.''

''I've got to meet someone,'' Ryder said. ''But I can be back by then. If you have enough.''

Paul gave a hearty laugh. ''Have you ever seen Anna plan anything small?''

Ryder laughed as well. ''No.''

''So don't worry about it then. Just come back.''

''Okay, I will.'' His gaze went to Brianna, and she thought she saw a special message deep in his eyes. ''I'll see you later.''

''All right,'' she husked. She sensed the knowing look exchanged by husband and wife.

Then he was gone and the room seemed to lose some of its intensity.

''Great-looking flowers,'' Paul commented, unaware of the shift of mood. ''Where did they come from?''

More sensitive to Brianna's feelings, Anna answered softly, ''From Brianna.'' Then shook her head at her husband when he was about to make a smart comment.

The conversation between the two of them was heard, but it was as if it were taking place in some other realm for Brianna. Her body was here, hearing, seeing, existing, but a part of her, a major part, was traveling somewhere else.

"Where do you suppose he's going?" she asked of no one in particular. It could have been a question posed only to herself.

"Lord knows with Ryder," Paul answered wryly.

Anna sought to smooth the situation. "Brianna, would you like something cold to drink? Paul has a client to see for a few minutes, so we can sit out on the patio and talk, just the two of us."

"I do?" Paul seemed startled.

"Yes, he called just before Brianna came."

"Oh! Oh, yes, he did. Mr....ah...Mr.... I've forgotten. But I'll remember." He paused. "I guess I'll see you two later then?"

"You'd better," Anna threatened, then frowned darkly to speed him on his way.

"Come on, Brianna. Let's go sit outside."

The patio was as friendly a place now as it had been the time before when she was there, and Brianna responded to its welcome with a long sigh that released pent-up tension. She still felt a bit unusual but that strange disjointedness seemed to have left her. She took a sip of lemonade and leaned her head against the back of the chair. Her lids fell shut to close out the light.

"Exactly how do you feel about Ryder?" Anna asked calmly at almost precisely that same instant.

Brianna sat up immediately, her green eyes wide with surprise, the liquid in her glass in danger of spilling.

"I don't understand," she denied, unease rushing back with force.

Anna smiled. "I'm not blind, Brianna."

"But I don't—"

"Okay, have it your way. But there are some things I think you ought to know before you get in too deeply." She took a moment to collect her thoughts. "Ryder is different from other men."

"So I've been told before."

For someone so small and so young, Anna knew how to summon a commanding presence. Her dark eyes flashed, and Brianna subsided.

"He's more like a brother to me than some of my own, so I can say this. Don't get involved with him too quickly, Brianna. You'll only get hurt if you do. Ryder... well, Ryder has hurt some women before you very badly. But it's not altogether his fault. They've asked for everything they've got."

"How?" Her throat was dry; she had a hard time formulating her words properly.

"They take him too seriously."

"You're—you're making him sound pretty bad."

Anna's eyes became sad. "I don't mean to." She leaned forward. "Look, I know we haven't known each other for all that long, but I like you and feel I should warn you. Ryder's had some pretty bad experiences in his life, and they've left him...full of scars.''

Brianna swallowed. "What kind of experiences?"

"His wife for one—you did know that he was married?''

Brianna nodded.

"She was a first-class bitch if I ever saw one! She never loved him—she just used him. I saw it, his family saw it, but he didn't. He was pretty young then—only twenty-two.''

"Were they married long?"

"Six years. And she made his life hell all the way through. I don't know how he put up with her!''

"Did—did they live in the house on King William Street?''

"No. His parents lived there then, and Susan would barely consent to visit it. There wasn't much love lost between her and Ryder's parents.

"When they finally divorced, Ryder was pretty bitter. Then his parents died...and his sister, and he felt responsible for all of their deaths. *He* was supposed to be the one to take Melissa back to Austin, but a job interview with the paper came up, his parents went instead...and they died coming back. When Melissa died too, I didn't think Ryder was going to make it. I—I won't go into all the details, that's for Ryder to tell, but he's convinced he could have prevented her death. If only she had come to him...told him...."

Brianna was silent, tears thick in her throat. She didn't tell Anna that she already knew.

"And since then he's kept himself distant from people—at least emotionally. His only involvement is through his column. We're his close friends, but that seems to be his limit. A few women have come and gone, but any feeling is always on their side. Not Ryder's." Anna looked at her with compassion. "I just wanted you to know," she finished softly.

Brianna could make no answer. She didn't know what to say. She could reassure Anna that she didn't have to worry about her, that she felt nothing. But it wouldn't be the entire truth and both of them would know it. Yet she wasn't in danger of being hurt too much. At least she didn't think she was. What she felt for Ryder was not a deep emotional thing. It was desire, which was pretty basic in itself, but it didn't touch the heart. At least she didn't think her heart was involved. No! Her heart was definitely not involved! He was interesting to her; possibly his very difference was what had attracted her in the first place. She had used the word fascinating before. Yes, he was fascinating. That was all. She could pull away any time that she wanted. So she didn't need to worry.

She could even leave for Pennsylvania tomorrow and never think of him again.

Chapter Seven

When Brianna saw Ryder once more, she knew her earlier avowal was a farce. He held a potent brand of appeal, and she was more than subject to it. He came unannounced into the kitchen where she was helping Anna cut pickles and tomatoes. She was chatting happily and was unaware of his presence until a long arm reached across in front of her and slipped a slice of pickle from its resting place on the tray.

Without even looking she knew whom that arm belonged to. And it definitely was not Paul. Slowly she turned about and drew a little breath because he had remained so close. Her fingers, still holding the knife, grazed the material of his shirt.

"Careful with that weapon, lady." His dark eyes were teasing. "I want to eat the meal not be part of it."

Brianna couldn't stop the excited leap of blood that was caused by his nearness. And she knew—she knew with blinding clarity—that she was past the point where she could leave and never give thought to him again. He was well and truly in her life, and she was going to have to think long and hard about what she was going to do about it. But to protect herself from these thoughts now, she retaliated by edging the point of the knife closer.

"Then put down that piece of pickle." She gave a pretend threat.

Ryder's sloping smile turned on Anna, who was watching their exchange with interest.

"It's your pickle—do I have to?"

Anna laughed and suggested, "I think I'd do what the lady says."

Ryder's gaze came back to Brianna, a devil lurking in their blueness. "I think I'll chance it." He flipped the slice into his mouth and after chewing it a few times, swallowed.

As Brianna witnessed this process, she wondered what she could do. He was calling her bluff! To get herself out of the situation with some sense of style, she pursed her lips and centered her attention on his midsection.

"Well, I could go in after it," she mused. "But that would be a bit messy and I wouldn't want to have to clean it up, so I'll let you get away with the crime this time, but don't try it again." She put the knife down on the counter.

That was the action Ryder seemed to be waiting for. He quickly reached for another slice, and taking advantage of her stunned look, bent his head and applied a swift kiss on her parted lips. Then he turned away laughing, enjoying the stolen tartness of his prize.

All Brianna could do was stare after him.

As had happened before when she was in the company of Paul and Anna, the afternoon passed quickly. And Ryder's presence only seemed to add to the happy haze.

They ate their hamburgers, deliciously cooked, not burned as Paul had kidded, and later made ice cream, using the old-fashioned, hand-cranked method instead of electric. Paul and Ryder took turns at the crank, both of them declaring that even though it was a lot of work, the finished product was definitely superior. And it was. Brianna had never tasted better.

The sun was beginning to set as the two women finished washing the last of the dessert dishes, and they could see from the kitchen window that the men were once again interested in the car.

"Ryder's a lot of help to us. He's saved us a bundle on car repairs. Paul's all thumbs when it comes to engines and such." Anna pushed a strand of dark hair away from her face and stretched her back a degree.

Brianna placed the drying towel on the small dish rack. They had decided to wash the few glass bowls and spoons instead of using the dishwasher. She watched as Anna moved slowly toward a chair.

"Are you feeling all right?" she asked, suddenly aware of the new lines of strain on Anna's face.

Anna gave a little shrug. "I feel pretty good for someone who's going to have a baby any minute."

Brianna blinked. She didn't know whether Anna was joking or if she was serious.

"Any minute?" she ventured.

"Well." Anna smiled wryly. "Any hour."

Brianna's mind was running back over the times she had been with Sylvia near the time of her deliveries.

"Are you having any pains?"

"I have been all afternoon."

"What?"

Anna grimaced slightly as if it had been nothing. "Just little ones, in my back."

"How far apart are they?"

"Getting closer."

"My Lord, Anna, why didn't you say something!"

"Because I didn't want to ruin a nice day."

"Having a baby is ruining a day?"

"Brianna," Anna said humorously, "we can debate that question all night, but if we do, you'd better get the hot water going, because I think we're going to need it." As she said this her face grew more strained. Then after a moment she said, "They're starting to get harder, and they've moved to my stomach."

"Oh my gosh!" Brianna hurried to the door. "Paul!" she called. "Paul, come quick! Anna's having the baby!"

At her anxious cry, Paul dropped the wrench he had been holding in preparation of giving it to Ryder and started to run toward the house.

As quickly as he could, Ryder scooted out from beneath the car, grabbed his shirt from the fender where he had left it, and ran toward the house as well.

Paul pushed past Brianna as if she weren't there in his hurry to get to his wife.

Anna's expression was lovely to behold as she gazed into her husband's anxious face.

"It's time, honey," she whispered.

Paul stood momentarily frozen, then shook himself back into action. "I'll get the suitcase," he stated gruffly and disappeared.

Within half a minute he was back. But as he hesitated in the middle of the room, the next step seemed to elude him. His brown eyes looked blank, and his carroty hair above paler than normal skin was in wild disarray, as if he had spent a couple of his seconds away running his hand agitatedly across his scalp.

"Paul?" Anna called softly, amusement mixed with love. "Don't forget me."

Paul's body gave an instant, very visible start, and Brianna wondered if he *had* forgotten her.

"Can you walk to the car?" he asked in a voice that sounded strange.

"Of course."

"Then I guess maybe we'd better go, huh?"

"I think we should."

He moved over to help Anna from the chair. Then after he had succeeded, stopped short and looked from Brianna to Ryder as if wondering if he should do something with them too.

Ryder helped him out. "We'll follow you to the hospital—unless you'd rather I drive you."

Paul shook his head. "No, I can."

"Okay, see you there. Good luck, squirt." He placed a fond kiss on Anna's cheek. She smiled back at him.

Even with everything that was happening, Brianna couldn't help being aware of Ryder. This was the first time she had seen him shirtless, except for that afternoon in Dallas, and then she had been so close she was doing more touching than looking.

His skin was a warm toasted brown all the way to the belt line of his jeans and seemed to have a natural sheen, which showed to best effect the contours of the muscles beneath. His shoulders were wide and strong looking, his chest deep and covered with a thin layer of dark body hair; his stomach was flat, almost ridged. There was not a speck of excess flesh. The jeans faithfully clung to his slim hips and strong muscular legs. Unconsciously Brianna moved a step closer.

Luckily for her, Ryder's attention was not centered on her so forcefully. He took her movement as a signal that she was ready to leave and, placing a hand at the small of her back, ushered her through the doorway, being sure to lock it behind them.

"Why don't we go in the Vette—there's no use taking both cars."

Mutely Brianna agreed. Lord, what was happening to her? This was no time to go off the deep end! Anna was about to have her baby—they needed to follow Paul to make sure he remembered his way to the hospital.

She couldn't say that she wasn't relieved when Ryder paused to replace his shirt before getting into the close confines of the car. She had herself under more control now, but she was still all shaky inside, and had to almost sit on her hands to ensure that they remained out of trouble.

For someone who had had a great deal of difficulties during the first trimester of her pregnancy, Anna delivered a beautiful little girl an amazingly short time later. Brianna, Ryder, and both sets of prospective grandparents had been sitting in the waiting room for barely an hour—Ryder having taken the time to call and give them the news that the baby was on its way—when a beaming Paul hurried in and announced the birth of his daughter.

She was beautiful, he exclaimed proudly, slapping Ryder on the back then hugging Brianna enthusiastically. Anna was doing fine; he hadn't been in the way at all during the birth as he had secretly feared—and he hadn't embarrassed himself by fainting. The entire process had been so beautiful, so efficiently done, how could he? he wondered, still existing on a plane somewhere other than the earthly one. And would they like to see the baby?

It was hard for Brianna not to beam with him and when she tilted her head to look at Ryder, she saw that he was smiling broadly with his friend as well.

"You better believe we want to see little Rebecca—that is the name you two decided on, isn't it?" Ryder asked.

"Rebecca," Paul repeated dreamily. "Yes."

"Is she ready yet?" Brianna questioned, having experienced the hospital process.

"The doctor told me I could bring you around to the viewing room in just a few minutes. If she's not there now, she soon will be!"

"Then what are we waiting for?" Ryder prompted.

The baby was everything Paul had said she was. She was sleeping, with a tiny little hand curled close to a pretty bowed mouth. She had a shock of dark black hair on a head that was smooth and round. Her nose was a small button and her skin was clear, not the least bit splotchy like some newborns. Brianna longed to reach out and touch her, but glass separated them and she had to content herself with just looking.

"I can't believe she's really here," Paul remarked softly, awe in his voice. "This morning it was just Anna and me and now...." Emotion clogged his throat.

A quick rush of tears came into Brianna's eyes. She could understand just exactly what Paul was saying. Empathy with other people's thoughts and feelings was one of the qualities that made her a good writer. She could *feel* without necessarily having experienced.

Something made her glance to her side and she saw that Ryder was looking at her, a strange expression marking his eyes. Brianna sniffed and tried to smile, but it was a watery effort and she turned away, embarrassed. He probably thought she was being stupid.

A half hour later, Brianna and Ryder left the hospital. They had been able to pay a short visit to Anna, who was exquisitely happy and proud to have produced such a child. But if the baby hadn't been perfect, Brianna knew that Anna would have been just as loving a mother—she was that kind of person. They stayed in the room for only a few minutes, silently agreeing to let Paul be alone with his wife, and Brianna never would forget the burning glow in his eyes.

Her chosen field was to be a writer dealing with love, and to witness it so closely, in its truest form, left her deeply impressed. She had her mother and father as an example, all the years they had chosen to remain together had only increased the love they felt; and her sister was happily married. But two of her brothers had not found much comfort in their marriages and the other was dead set against anything that even looked as if it might end up in a trip to the altar. So she knew both sides of the love coin and knew how rare total commitment was to find.

Darkness was surrounding them as Ryder directed his car through the hospital parking lot and out onto the street. It was not very late—only about ten—but it felt much later. Brianna gave a long sigh, the emotional high she had been experiencing ebbing away to be replaced by a quiet tiredness.

Ryder glanced across at her. "It's been a long day," he observed.

"For everyone," she agreed.

He was silent for a moment. "I'm glad everything worked out okay for Paul and Anna."

"Me too."

She felt his eyes come to rest on her once again. "Why? You barely know them."

A little of Brianna's tiredness went away as she tried to decide just what he meant. She had the crazy feeling that in some way he was testing her.

"It's true that I haven't known them long," she affirmed carefully. "But sometimes it doesn't take an age to decide that you like someone and want the best for them."

Again he was silent. Then he said softly, "You can open yourself up for a lot of hurt that way."

They were delicately fencing on two levels—he, from his experiences, and she, from hers. "You can," she agreed after a second of serious thought. "But, to me, if you close yourself off just on the chance that someone *might* hurt you, you're doing yourself more harm than anyone else ever could."

She could sense that his fingers had tightened on the steering wheel. She knew what she was doing, what she was saying. She remembered Anna's confidence. But that was her view and he could accept it, or not accept it, as he pleased.

"You've never been hurt very badly before, have you, Brianna?"

"No."

"So you don't know what you're talking about."

She decided to challenge him, pretend that she didn't have any knowledge of the horror of his marriage. "Do you?"

He gave a harsh laugh that vibrated within her. "I'll say I do."

"Do you want to talk about it?" she asked, hoping that he would, not out of curiosity, but because she felt that he needed to.

"No."

Brianna gazed at his profile as he guided the car

along the busy streets. She tried for lightness, hoping it might take some of the harshness from his features.

"Confession's good for the soul," she prompted.

"Not when what caused the upset is long dead and buried."

"But is it dead and buried?"

"Have you always fancied yourself a psychologist?"

"No, but I understand people."

"Or like to think you do."

"What are you talking about?" Suddenly she didn't feel quite so assured.

"I could hurt you."

Brianna's pulse stopped for a moment at his quietly stated words. "I'd have to let you," she responded, a tightening in the region of her stomach the result of rising tension.

"You wouldn't have anything to say about it."

"Why are you so sure?"

"Because I know the way your body reacts to mine."

The journey from tired contentedness to jangling wariness had been a short one. Struggling for refuge Brianna countered, "I could hurt you too."

"I doubt it."

Anger at his stubborn disavowal made her claim, "I'm not stupid! I know you respond to me too!"

"You're a beautiful woman."

"That's not all it is!"

"That's what you'd like to think."

"What makes you so sure it's not the same for me?

You're not exactly repulsive!" Never, as they had walked companionably through the hospital doors, had she expected that they would enter into such a conversation.

"I appreciate your vote of confidence." His eyes left the road to run over her appreciatively, a glitter that was not a reflection of the passing lights lighting their depths.

"And I yours!" No matter what, she was not going to let him have the last word.

A few minutes passed before he asked, "Do you want to test it out?"

"Test what out?" She had been caught off guard.

"The theory that what we feel for each other is just... physical need?"

Brianna felt herself thrust into a situation that was fast racing out of her hands, if it had ever been in them!

"I—"

"My apartment isn't far from here."

Brianna swallowed. She truly didn't know what to say. This wasn't the first proposition she had received, but she had never before been asked with quite so much cold calculation.

"I promise I won't write about it," he added silkily, "if you'll do the same."

He still thought the love scenes in her book were extensions of her own experiences! He thought she was promiscuous, had done so from the beginning. And her letting him get so close to her that first day had only imbedded that fact in his mind.

Brianna decided to call a halt right then and there. She was opening her mouth to tell him his mistake, no matter how much ridicule he might heap on her, when she realized he had taken her silence as an affirmative answer. He was smiling—a purely villainous smile—and he pressed down harder on the accelerator, making the car jump forward to cover ground more quickly.

"No, Ryder, I didn't mean..." she began when he interrupted.

"Don't you believe what you said earlier? You said to close yourself off from people and experiences would only hurt you, or words to that effect."

"But I didn't mean—"

"Then you take back what you said?"

Brianna's chin firmed. "No." Maybe she was going about this the wrong way. Maybe she should agree to do as he said. Sitting back and doing nothing had got her nowhere. She subsided in her protests. She had assured herself that she didn't feel any stronger emotion for him than desire, maybe making love with him and getting it over with would release her from the spell he seemed to have thrown over her. Maybe her first inclination, the day they met, had been right. She said nothing more and forced her mind into an unfeeling blank. She wasn't going to debate right or wrong. She was just going to do it, damn it!

Ryder's apartment was a studio set in a small exclusive complex. It was tastefully decorated, revealing a liking for strong accent colors.

Brianna walked into the living room with seeming calm. Waiting at the hospital in shorts was one thing, there hadn't been time to change. But here, in Ryder's lair, she felt distinctly at a disadvantage. But she couldn't show her vulnerability. She had to tough it out.

"Very nice," she applauded verbally, her gaze going over the burnt-orange walls and cream-colored molding.

He made a negligent gesture. "It's home."

Brianna ran a finger along a leather cushion of the couch as she walked behind it on her way to take a seat.

"Would you like something to drink?" he asked blandly, so much so in fact that she wondered if he was thinking the same as she about the oldness of the line.

Yet ancient though it was, Brianna clung to it with both hands. "Yes, I would. What do you have?"

Ryder moved to a cabinet that was set against one wall. "Whatever you want."

"I'll take a Scotch."

"With water or soda?"

"Straight," Brianna replied levelly, knowing that she would need some aid to get through this experience.

He turned to look at her, one eyebrow raised. "I didn't think you drank all that much."

Brianna returned his look. "I do sometimes."

He shrugged. "Okay. Whatever you say."

He came to the couch carrying the two drinks. His

looked exactly the same as hers so she decided he must be drinking a Scotch as well.

He handed a glass to her and she took it. How she maintained the rock steadiness of her hand, she would never know.

She took a sip and almost choked but forced herself not to reveal it in any way.

He lifted the glass to his lips and took a satisfactory swallow. She could feel his eyes going over her, touching her by now tumbled hair, her face—especially her lips—and then moving down to the rounded curves of her breasts as they pushed against the material of her thin shirt.

Then he surprised her by saying, "I read your book."

"Yes, I know."

He grimaced slightly, remembering the article. "I'd forgotten." He took another drink. "I liked it."

Brianna rested the glass in her free palm, while keeping her fingers wrapped about the damp coolness. "And did that surprise you?"

"Frankly? Yes."

"Why?" She knew it was only putting off the inevitable, but if he wanted to talk, she definitely knew that she did too.

"Because I'd never read a romance before."

"Too prejudiced?"

"No, I'd just never picked one up."

"What did you like about it?"

"Your style. The way you wove your words."

"For a newspaperman that's quite a compliment."

"We're not all so vicious in deleting our adjectives."

"It's your editors who are."

"Sometimes."

Brianna smoothed her fingers along the edge of the glass. "Would you read another one?"

"Of yours?"

"I suppose."

"Yes." He finished his drink and placed it on a side table, yet he made no move to come closer to her. "Something else surprised me about your book."

"What?"

"That the hero and heroine were faithful to each other."

"My hero and heroine always are."

."Hmmm." He began to play with a long fly-away strand of her hair, winding it loosely around his finger. "I always thought that in the kind of books you write they sleep with as many people as possible."

Brianna tried not to notice what he was doing. "Some writers have done that in the past—written books like that. But that's not what I want to do. I write about love between a certain man and a certain woman. If they sleep around, then they're not in love, not in the real sense of the word."

"But you don't mind them sleeping with each other— or rather, doing a lot of *not* sleeping with each other."

Brianna moved uneasily. "No."

His fingers let the strand of hair fall back into place. But they soon followed and she felt his palm run along the back of her head. She trembled slightly.

"Are you seriously involved with anyone right now?"

Her throat was tight. "I told you before, just my cat."

"I wasn't sure you were telling the truth."

His hand began to burrow beneath the weight of her hair toward her neck. A rush of chills ran up and down her spine.

"I was." Her reply was delayed.

"I find that hard to believe."

How could someone have such a smoky, sexy voice? It wasn't fair! It did something wonderful to her system, and yet at the same time, she knew she should be afraid.

"What—what about you? Are you involved with anyone right now?"

"No."

"I find that hard to believe too."

He shrugged. "No one interests me—or at least, no one did."

Brianna's breathing was becoming restricted. It was going to happen soon now. She felt her gaze being drawn as if by a magnet and slowly turned her head. Without her being aware of it he had moved closer. She could feel his soft exhalations of breath on her cheek, could smell the warmth of liquor, could see the tiny lines at the sides of his eyes and the fine texture of his tanned skin. Her eyes then came to rest on his and she became lost in their deep blue allure.

Almost in slow motion her fingers came up to touch the line of his jaw. He turned his head and kissed the inside of her palm. Then once again he met her look and removed the glass from her unprotesting grasp.

Brianna took a shallow, audible breath, her body coming alive to the stirring sensation of anticipatory pleasure, her emerald eyes wide and waiting.

Ryder didn't leave her in suspense for long. At the same instant that his arms wound around her, pulling her to him, his lips fastened onto hers—languid, experienced, demanding a return of his cool passion.

But within Brianna, there was no room for cold, sophisticated response. In her there was only a sense of intoxicating hunger—a growing need that had nothing to do with the small amount of distilled liquid she had earlier tasted.

His lips were like warm, soft honey. The more she tasted, the more she wanted. She placed her arms about his neck and returned the increasing pressure. She molded her body to his, her breasts flattening against the wall of muscles in his chest, sensitive to the heart that beat strongly beneath the soft material of his shirt.

Her ardor was Ryder's undoing. If he had intended a clinical assessment conducted with deliberate passion, his aim soon changed. Holding the vibrant, yielding, passionate form that was Brianna seemed to override whatever structure he had mentally paced for them. His caressing hands soon began a more intent exploration of her shape, following the curve of her back to her narrow waist and slimly rounded hips. Her delectable thighs were next discovered, the skin like satin in its smoothness and softness. He couldn't seem to get enough of touching her! It was as if he needed to become familiar with her every inch. His hand passed over her ribs in the process of gaining the full curve of her breast, his fingertips seeking and finding a hardening nipple, at first teasing it, and then moving so that his entire hand strained to cover the swelling mass of aroused flesh.

All the while his mouth seemed intent on devouring hers, crushing hers, forcing her head back until it was only the strength of his arm that kept her from falling backward. Then his arm released its firm hold and she was lowered against the cushions of the couch, his body moving to imprison her beneath him. Only at that moment did he release her lips.

Ryder's eyes were lighted by a deep burning fire when he looked at her, a slumberous glow that she knew was intense desire. She didn't need the confirmation of his words, but a thrill shot through her when he husked lowly, "I want you, Brianna St. Clair."

Brianna didn't need experience to tell her what came next. She had written of it many times. So she wasn't surprised when he began to unbutton the front of her blouse and unclasp the front catch of her bra. A swiftly taken catch of indrawn breath showed his appreciation of what his actions had revealed.

When his mouth came down to touch the bounty, she arched her back and gave a soft moan, carried away on a cloud of intense longing.

It was when his hands lowered and began the job of undoing the button and zip to her shorts that she experienced her first qualm of inhibition. She moved so that the action would be difficult for him, unconsciously trying to take his mind away from its intended path by bringing his mouth back to hers. Her parted lips were more than successful. His arms rose to bring her to him as if she were already a part of him, her body intensely aware of his every inch—the hard pressure of his manhood tight against her hips. His tongue invaded the silken smoothness of her mouth, and this time she didn't pull away; this time she welcomed its presence. A dizzying sensation of passion crowded all other thought from her mind. She wanted him—she needed him! She didn't care if, to him, this was some kind of experiment. Her fingernails curved into the heated skin of his back, ignoring the material of his shirt.

At first she didn't understand the slurred words he murmured, his mouth nuzzling the soft curve of her neck. Then, when he repeated the short directive, she comprehended.

"Take it off."

Brianna was trembling as she complied by lifting the tail of the pullover from beneath his belt and bringing it up over his spine.

He moved so that the shirt could be easily removed. Then, still balanced with one knee on either side of her thighs, he brought one of her hands up to the nakedness of his chest.

"Touch me," he requested softly, and a tingling started to rapidly course its way through her body as her fingers began to curl in a section of the dark spiraling hair that grew on his bronzed skin. Then as her hand began to move, reveling in the intimate act he had bid her do, he gave a low, ragged groan and pushed his weight away from herself and the couch.

Brianna continued to lay there, momentarily stunned. She didn't know what was happening. Was he stopping again? Had she done something that repulsed him, that made him not want her any longer? Her eyes were dark with confusion as she looked up and across at him.

But immediately upon meeting his melting gaze, she knew that a waning of passion was not the cause. If anything, he looked to be even more caught up in his sensual urges than before.

"My bedroom's up there," he murmured huskily, motioning to a curving set of stairs, before holding his hand out to her.

For a moment Brianna did nothing. Then, shyly, she extended her hand and felt his fingers wrap warmly around her own.

He lifted her from the couch and, as she stood before him, pushed the rest of the material of her blouse and bra away from her shoulders, letting them fall carelessly onto the carpet beside his shirt.

His eyes held an appreciative gleam as he whispered thickly, "Beautiful." But he made no attempt to touch her. Instead, he turned and began to pull her toward the stairs.

Brianna swallowed tightly as she followed. She knew if she told him this was her first time he wouldn't believe her. So she silently took each step and tried to strengthen her mental resolution. The world was full of firsts—first words, first steps, first dates, first kisses—this would be no different. She was with the man she wanted to be with. The man she had awaited for so long.

Ryder's bedroom was surprisingly austere. Again there was the use of color, but there were few useless decorative additions. The main occupant of the room was a large king-size bed with a throw spread of white fabric. With one sweeping motion Ryder rid the bed of its cover and then turned back to Brianna.

He smiled that little lazy smile of his, the one she liked so much, and closed the short distance between them.

"I think we're still a little too dressed for the occasion, don't you?" he drawled softly and reached out to grasp her waist, his thumbs moving on the lower side curves of her breasts.

Now was the time Brianna needed all the assurance of vast experience—not just the instructional value of being widely read—because doing something like this was not exactly the same thing as reading about doing it, or writing about it, for that matter! She didn't know whether he wanted her to finish undressing by herself or wait for him to do it. And what about him? Did she undress him? What exactly was the procedure he wanted her to follow? Most of the time in her books, the heroine was so swept away by passion that she had no time to think. But that wasn't the way it was with her now. Oh, she was still tremendously aware of him. But the trip upstairs had allowed a taste of apprehension to seep into her mind and she couldn't seem to shake it.

At her hesitation and almost imperceptible stiffening, a puzzled little frown descended on Ryder's brow.

"What's the matter? Is something wrong?" he asked.

"No, nothing." Her voice was high, tight, but it must have been convincing because his smile deepened and he bent his head to kiss her.

Again the sweetness of his kiss was like a fine wine to Brianna—the pureness of discovery, of taste. But even though he began to caress her, his kisses moving from her lips to her throat to her ear and back again, his fingers smoothly covering her breasts and stroking them, this time she couldn't become lost to herself enough to totally respond. The bed was too near; what they were going to do too close!

Ryder's hands moved once again to the catch of her shorts.

Brianna was breathing hard, her trepidation increasing, and when she felt the catch give, she instantly pulled away, causing his fingers to slip off the zip before it was completely undone.

His frown was more ingrained as Ryder pulled back a space.

Brianna attempted a smile while her trembling fingers were at the back of her shorts trying to span the gap, but it didn't come off very well. She was beginning to feel like a stupid virginal idiot! And if she could have managed to kick herself, she would have done it. She was acting like a fool! But she couldn't seem to stop.

"Would you like to tell me what's going on with you?" he asked in a deceptively soft voice.

"I— I—"

Excellent! Now she was stammering! She could have stepped straight from the pages of a Barbara Cartland novel!

"Are you trying to pay me back?"

At that Brianna gave an uncomprehending stare.

"For the time I cut out on you," he explained.

All at once she realized what he was talking about. She started to tell him his mistake, but he didn't give her enough time.

A touch of anger had entered his voice when he went on to warn, "Because if that's your idea, you can forget it! I didn't want to take unfair advantage of you then, but this time we both knew what we were getting in to from the beginning. There's not going to be any changing of minds or backing out. You made a deal and you're going to keep it."

For a moment all Brianna could do was continue to stare at him, her eyes looking to take up most of the space of her face. Then she instinctively began to back away.

She had taken only a couple of steps when Ryder made a mockery of the distance she had put between them and stopped all possibility of further retreat by lashing out and drawing her against him.

For only the second time in their relationship, Brianna experienced a sense of fear. The first had been

when she didn't know him all that well yet was taking
him to her hotel room, and now, when she knew him
a little better, but had never before suffered his anger.

If she had been in a more stable frame of mind, she
would have thought to hide it. But, being in the state
she was, her fear was very evident for him to see.

Ryder's eyes were blazing as he looked down at
her, still caught up in his perception of her recanting
on their agreement, but as he continued to look at
her, some of the heat left his gaze and the grip of his
fingers on her upper arms loosened.

"You're afraid of me?" he asked in wonder, as if
unable to believe that she could be.

Brianna's face was immediately flooded with crimson, her fright melting in the face of his incredulity.
Miserably, she was aware that because of her inexperience she had mishandled the entire situation. If only
she could have overcome her stupid, naïve nervousness!

"You are!" Now it was Ryder's turn to be confused.

Brianna could sense his mind working behind his
frowning mask. And to add to her embarrassment, he
eventually came up with an accurate assessment of
the situation.

Slowly, he questioned, "You've never done this before, have you?" He shook his head, as if trying to
clear it. "No—that's stupid. You write about sex all
the time. You've got to have the experience to back
it." Then he stopped. "Haven't you?" His blue eyes

became even more intent. "Brianna, you *have* slept with a man before...."

Brianna tried to turn away, to hide her face. She didn't want him to see her any longer. She didn't want him to know. But he forced her to look back at him.

"Haven't you?" he demanded, impatiently giving her a little shake.

Tears formed in Brianna's eyes as she stared back at him. They clogged her throat. But he was waiting for an answer and looked as if he was prepared to wait forever. Finally she choked out a strangled "No."

"Oh, my God!" Regret flooded his expression and his eyes took on a haunted look. Unknowingly his fingers tightened their grip. Then a harshness entered his gaze and he dropped his hands as if suddenly burned. "Why the hell didn't you tell me?"

Brianna's fighting spirit picked itself up from the dust at her feet and rallied to save her pride. "Just what was I supposed to do?" she snapped. "Wear a sign around my neck that said *Virgin*?"

Ryder glared at her for a moment, then agreed, "That might have helped!"

"Who?" she demanded.

"Unsuspecting men."

"Well, bully for all unsuspecting men! We can't have them making a mistake, can we?"

Brianna's emerald gaze was flashing as she tenaciously hid behind one strong emotion to avoid another. Her hands had come up to rest on her slim hips as she railed; and she was unconscious of the picture she made, standing topless, wearing only a pair of brief red shorts.

But even in his disturbed state that had nothing to do with arousal, Ryder was aware and moved over to his closet to withdraw a shirt. He threw it to her.

"Here—cover yourself up."

Crimson flags once again flew on the curves of her cheeks. She had totally forgotten her state of undress. Wordlessly she slipped into the freshly laundered white shirt. It hung on her to a degree, made to stretch over Ryder's more muscular build, but at least it didn't swallow her as it would have if he had been a larger man.

"That's better," he decided when she had successfully closed the last button.

Brianna's chin lifted. "Thank you."

Some of the tension that had mounted in the room was disappearing, and a return of the little mocking smile Ryder had earlier used came back to pull at his lips. "After you?" He held his hand out toward the stairs.

Brianna's nemesis in always wanting to have the last word prompted her to say, "What's the matter? Now that you know my deadly secret, aren't you interested anymore?"

Ryder's blue eyes ran the course of her body, making her wonder at her sanity. She was being released from the insane agreement. Did she really want him to change his mind? At least, right now?

Finally when he spoke, his tone was softly musing. "Let's just say that the timing isn't right."

"I could go out and get some experience. It wouldn't be all that hard to find."

"Do you want to do that?"

"Not really."

"Then don't. Not on my account anyway."

For some unknown reason that last sentence hurt. Not on his account—was she so inconsequential to him that he didn't want her to make the effort?

Stiffly Brianna moved to the stairs and started down. This had to have been one of the worst days in her entire life! Not even the arrival of the baby could save it. She should have stayed at home, in bed, curled up with a good history book!

The sight of her blouse and bra crumpled on the floor was not a happy one for Brianna. She bent to retrieve them and after she raised up, met Ryder's amused expression.

Not for the world was she going to blush. She had blushed enough lately to last a lifetime. She was *not* going to do it again! Through force of will she held his gaze and dared him to make a comment.

When he didn't, she said tightly, "Where can I change?"

"In there." He pointed to a doorway along a short hall.

Brianna found that it was a small bathroom. Quickly she changed back into her clothing and folded the shirt. Yet she hesitated before going back out. It wasn't that she didn't want to see him again, or that she was ashamed of her inexperience. It was just that she hated to be an object of his ridicule, although to be fair, he hadn't made fun of her. He had been angry, he had been surprised, but he hadn't laughed.

Oh, Lord, if he had laughed!

Brianna straightened her shoulders and retraced her steps to the living room.

"I'm ready," she announced coolly, handing him the neatly arranged shirt.

"All right." He took it from her and placed it on the edge of a wide bookshelf, where to her amazement, the book she had autographed for him was placed in between onyx bookends along with a few other paperbacks.

She forced her eyes away and marched to the door. She was thankful that he had taken the time to don his shirt as well. Now, maybe, as he drove her back to the Daniels's so that she could pick up her car, she could pretend that this little fiasco had never happened. She could try to convince herself that they were coming straight from the hospital. But as she thought those words she knew they were hopeless. This night would be forever indelibly imprinted on her mind.

Chapter Eight

Brianna spent the next week totally immersing herself in her work. She endured long hours at the institute library and at the small library located on the Alamo grounds as well. But even though she was gathering reams of information, she wasn't enjoying it. And she knew the cause had nothing to do with her external actions. Her main complaint was entirely emotional.

Not even a short trip over to Paul's and Anna's to see little Rebecca helped. The entire time she was there, she was afraid that the cause of her trouble was going to pop in at any moment—just as he had the last two times she was there. So she didn't allow herself the pleasure of relaxation, and was stupidly disappointed when, as she was leaving, Ryder still had made no appearance.

And it was that very disappointment that unsettled her the most. Was she going insane? She couldn't seem to erase him from her mind. No matter how hard she tried, he was always there.

It wasn't as if they had parted on friendly terms either. After she left his apartment, not one word had been exchanged between them—not even when she had let herself out of his car and walked with stiffly held, proud shoulders the short distance to her own parked car. She would be damned if she was going to show the confusion she felt inside! And he seemed just as determined not to want to try to force her.

And in the time that followed, her confusion only became worse. Sometimes she almost hated him. Why had he come into her life? She didn't need him. She didn't want him. Well, at least she didn't now. And yet, she did. At the least opportune moments, remembrance of their closeness sprang upon her consciousness. Sometimes it was so vivid she wanted to scream. But the women who ran the quiet, dignified Alamo library would have been startled quite out of their wrinkling skin if she had. So she contained herself, but her suppression didn't make for pleasant thoughts. And when one of the nice ladies came over to inquire politely if she needed further assistance, Brianna actually growled at her. Immediately she apologized. But the incident was further proof that she was in a bad way.

The following Monday as Brianna came to grudging late morning awareness, it was also to the realization that her doorbell was being rung. The one ring was soon followed by another. Brianna groaned as she slid her feet from beneath the sheet. Who in the world?

As she struggled downstairs, her arm groped for the sleeve of her robe and she ran her fingers through the long blond strands of her hair, hoping to bring them to some order. She pulled the robe tightly about her waist before reaching out to unlock the door. Then her hand paused; she wasn't about to let just anyone in, so she called huskily, "Who is it?"

"Who would you like it to be?"

With a combined flip of both stomach and heart Brianna recognized Ryder's voice.

"What do you want?" she asked. It was the only thing she could think of to say, and she despaired that she had sounded so ineffectual. She should be cool, dismissing, but it was too early in the morning and she had been thrown totally off guard.

"To see you."

Brianna swallowed. "Why?"

At that Ryder paused.

"To give you something?"

His answer was a question.

"What?"

"Open the door and find out."

"But I'm not dressed!"

She could almost feel his amusement through the thick wood and could have lashed herself for her stupidity. She had really laid herself open for that one and she wasn't surprised when he responded, "All the better."

Brianna took a bracing breath. She firmed her voice. "I didn't mean it that way."

"Then let me in."

"I didn't invite you."

"So?"

"So go away!"

"Maybe what I have to give you has something to do with the fact that I own this house."

Brianna was silent a moment, her fingers clutching

her robe together over her breast, remaining where they had flown the instant she heard Ryder's reply.

"Slip it under the door."

"It won't fit."

"Oh...!" Brianna's answer was colored by rising impotent annoyance, whether with him or herself she wasn't sure. "Go see about some of your other 'properties.' A long time ago you told me you dabbled in real estate. I haven't seen much evidence of it yet." There. She had been wondering about that for a long time. All he ever seemed to do was irritate her and write his column in the newspaper.

"My 'property' can take care of itself."

"Are you sure it exists?"

"A number of construction firms believe in it."

"Are they building a mental institution for you?"

"No, a shopping center."

"A shopping center?"

"Just outside of downtown. It's something I got involved in a few years ago with a few friends."

"It sounds lucrative."

"It's just a small center. Listen, I'm getting tired of talking to the door."

"Bye."

She heard him give a deep sigh. "Brianna..."

"Oh, all right, if I have to see you. Could you come back in ten minutes?"

"I already know what you look like in—what's the term?—dishabille."

At that, and the laughter in his voice, Brianna flicked the lock and swept the door open, her green eyes snapping as she warned, "If you're expecting *early orgy*, you're in for a disappointment!"

Ryder looked momentarily disconcerted as his eyes ran over her, taking in the baby-blue cotton pajama pants jutting from beneath her functional blue cotton robe. He did a double take at the fuzzy slippers that made her small feet seem twice their normal size.

"I wear what's comfortable," she defended herself, even though she knew she didn't have to.

"I know of something that's a lot more comfortable."

"I don't want to know about it," she interrupted.

His blue eyes danced. "I think you already do."

"And it has nothing to do with wearing anything, am I correct?"

"I told you you already knew."

Brianna's chin lifted. She was the insane one for ever letting him in!

She took a moment to let her gaze go over him. He was dressed in another pair of jeans, navy cords this time, and a cream short sleeved shirt. In his hand was a tiny collection of yellow and white daisies. He held them out toward her.

"I came to give these to you," he said softly, causing Brianna's gaze to become imprisoned by his. "And to ask if you'd like to come with me to visit El Mercado."

"El Mercado?" God! She was becoming an echo machine!

"The Mexican Market. It's like a giant flea market — whatever you want, they've got it there."

Brianna just continued to stare while her mind worked overtime. He was here! Standing right before her! Asking her to go out with him again—after what had happened! What did it mean? Should she go? Was she afraid to go? No, that was idiotic.

"When?"

"Is anything wrong with right now?"

Brianna detached her eyes. She looked down at herself. "I'd have to change."

Ryder laughed softly. "I'd hope so."

Brianna knew she should say no. He was too darned assured... of himself... of her! But the word wouldn't pass her lips.

"Take all the time you need," he advised, "I'm in no hurry." His gaze moved about the hall until it settled on a small, decorative glass container on a corner shelf unit next to the stairs. Without another word, he moved to pluck it from its position and turned to walk toward the kitchen, taking the daisies with him.

Brianna continued to look after his departing back until he moved out of sight. Then she shook herself. Why was it every time he was near, everything seemed so simple? And yet, when she was alone, everything was so complex? If she didn't know better, she would say that she was falling in love with him.

Quickly she put that thought far, far away from her mind. She was much too sensible to do anything as foolish as that—especially when she had been warned.

As Ryder had told her, the Mexican Market contained a little of whatever anyone could possibly want. There were even suits of armor there, as well as piñatas, wicker baskets, embroidered dresses, shirts, leather goods, all kinds of jewelry, a bootmaker, even large crepe-paper flowers in a rainbow of colors that had their origins in Mexico—and each section was tended by the proprietor of their allotted area. The building the market was in wasn't much more than an old warehouse, and a multitude of fans kept the air stirring a degree to help lower the stifling heat.

Brianna was admiring an artisan's rendition of a tree in metal sculpture when Ryder brought her attention to another artist's ware: copies of pen and ink drawings of the old San Antonio missions. Immediately Brianna became engrossed in the drawings.

"I'm having a sale today," the booth operator told her in a heavily accented voice. "A Monday special. Two for nine dollars."

"Did you do these?" she asked, her green eyes raising to his. He was a tall, thin man somewhere in his forties with short black hair and black eyes.

"A friend of mine did them."

"They're very nice." The admiration in her tone showed she was about to agree.

"We'll give you three," Ryder preempted her acceptance.

Brianna looked at him in surprise, her hand partway to her purse.

"They could sell for at least fifteen!" the man countered.

Then Ryder said something in Spanish that caused the operator to sit forward in his chair and fire something back. All Brianna could do was watch in amazement. She had never thought about it, but living in San Antonio with its Mexican flavor and its location so close to the border, a number of its citizens must be bilingual.

Finally, when the debate was settled, Ryder directed her to hand over five dollars. Mutely Brianna did and the proprietor happily wrapped her selections in a protective plastic covering.

When they started to walk away, Ryder gave her shoulders a gentle squeeze. "They're worth maybe two dollars apiece—giving him a pretty good markup. But five for both isn't too bad. Did you mind me giving in?"

Brianna turned her head to look at him. "I would have given him the nine."

"And deprived him of a chance to bargain?"

"Was that what you were doing? I thought you were browbeating the poor man."

"He held his own pretty well—he got the extra dollars."

"Was that why he was smiling?"

"I suppose. But maybe he was just happy to have someone as beautiful as you witness his performance."

A compliment?

"Hmmm." Brianna paused to pretend an interest in the details of the leather working on a saddle.

Just how much of what he was saying could she consider as genuine?

His hand came out to cover hers, trapping it against the smooth leather. "You are beautiful, Brianna."

Brianna couldn't stop her gaze from lifting up to meet the dark intensity of his. They were in a quiet corner, the hum of the fan a short distance away making the wooden wind chimes hanging above their heads clatter pleasantly in its breeze, and the rest of the people crowding the building seemed to be everywhere else but where they were. They were alone, as alone as any two people could be in a public place.

When Ryder's lips first touched hers, Brianna experienced a sweet rush of remembered enjoyment. Then as the sensation began to deepen along with the kiss, she drew back in startled awareness. Twice she had been rejected by this man. Was she going to let herself be put in that position so easily again?

Unconsciously Brianna shook her head, then her eyes locked with his, and she saw a seriousness she had never seen in them before.

"You do strange things to me, lady," Ryder observed huskily. "Wonderful things." His arms were still around her waist. "Maybe that's why I can't seem to leave you alone."

Brianna's heart was still beating rapidly from their earlier closeness, but it jumped into a faster pace at his unexpected words. Then, before she could act to control it, a spontaneous question left her lips.

"Do you try?"

The lazy smile appeared on his well-drawn mouth. "Like hell! But it hasn't seemed to do any good."

A pleasurable pain shot through Brianna. Her forearms were resting on his chest; her hips pulled tightly against his. She was conscious of the intimacy of her contact with him.

Was it possible that he wasn't quite as detached as she had thought the last time they had been together? Had he been using the method of cool seduction as a way of getting her out of his system, just as she had made the decision to stop fighting herself and do essentially the same with him? Had they both been tilting at the same windmill of attraction only to emerge together in inglorious defeat?

"Are you going to keep trying?" She couched her request with seeming ease, when, in fact, her entire body was one gigantic mass of inwardly trembling protoplasm. For some inexplicable reason, she had the instinctive feeling that these few seconds could be the most important in her life.

"I'm not sure," he decided gruffly, a frown settling on his forehead, darkening his features.

A tremulous smile lighted Brianna's lips and eyes. "I don't bite," she reassured him.

The frown went away a degree as his deep blue eyes developed faint crinkles at their edges. "No, but you could do something much worse."

"What?" Brianna breathed, hoping for something she didn't fully understand, just knowing that she desperately needed to know. The sensuous heat emanating from his body was making her head begin to swim.

Ryder remained silent, his gaze seeming to attempt a probe of her soul.

Brianna's knees felt wobbly. No one had ever looked at her in such a way before. It was as if he were searching for something within her, something essential, something he had to find before he could commit himself.

"I'm afraid I could come to love you."

The sentence was so softly spoken Brianna could have missed it if she had been any less attentive. As it was, alive to his every breath, she heard. It didn't matter that they were no longer as alone as they once had been...that people were now milling about in the aisles close by...that they were the object of more than one pair of curious eyes as customers moved slowly along. She understood. And suddenly, like a blinding flash of white-hot illumination, she understood herself as well.

What she felt for Ryder wasn't merely attraction. It didn't exist on purely a physical plane. She loved him. She didn't know when it had happened, when attraction had changed into something more. But it had. Her inward tumult quaked its way into outward expression and she knew Ryder was able to feel her trembling.

Yet, she could say nothing about how she felt. Her revelation was too new, and she was very much conscious that he had said he was "afraid" that he "could" come to love her. He hadn't said that he did. Or that he wanted to.

Brianna took an unsteady breath. Then Ryder's head dipped to place a light kiss on her parted lips. "Don't worry about it," he advised gently, taking the necessity of a response from her hands. "It's my problem. I'll deal with it."

Deal with it? What was he going to do? Try to kill

any emotion that might happen to be born? That realization was not very reassuring on the heels of her own discovery.

Brianna didn't resist when Ryder turned and began to pull her along. The pressure of his fingers was firm on her own; they were the only thing she had to cling to in a world that had suddenly decided to escape from its humdrum existence in a boring orbit and thrust itself willy-nilly into space, leaving its inhabitant dazed by the spectacular leap into the unknown.

Lying in bed that night Brianna was still suffering from the aftereffects of the shock she had given herself. Was it possible that she loved him? Yes, it was possible. It was more than possible! She did! Yet, why hadn't she seen it, recognized her confusion for what it was? She was the big, famous romance writer. Love was her occupation in a sense. She spent her days thinking up plots that furthered that immortal feeling. And then she had to be practically hit between the eyes before she could recognize that same emotion in herself.

Brianna gave a dry, unamused chuckle. There really must be something to the story about the cobbler's children having no shoes...and the old saying about taking a busman's holiday. It seemed that whenever someone did something well and constantly, they developed a kind of superficial blindness to those close to them—their compulsion was turned inward.

However, now she knew. So what was she going to

do about it? She could never admit it. Not to Ryder. Anna had told her he had been hurt badly by love and he had later confirmed that fact himself. And, as well, Anna had told her about the women who had been hurt by him—that they had tried to get too close to him, had made the mistake of becoming involved when he had nothing to give. Had she stupidly let herself fall into the same position?

But, no. Her case was different. Ryder was the one who first spoke of love, even if he had done it grudgingly, without admitting to it. That proved the idea had crossed his mind. He had as much as confessed his vulnerability to her. Could she take advantage of that?

One of her heroines would. She would make the hero come to love her. An idea began to form in Brianna's brain. With all her practice writing involved story lines, why couldn't she write one for herself? She knew life wasn't as easy to control as the pages of a book, but if she drafted several scenarios. . . .

The next morning Brianna set about implementing the plans for her next chapter. And she was happy with what she came up with. First, she would have a dinner party; she would invite Ryder, along with Anna and Paul, using the excuse that she wanted to pay them back for all the hospitality they had shown her. Little Rebecca would be old enough to come. That would be bait for Ryder. And she would make her specialty: stuffed pork chops. He wouldn't be able to resist!

With a happy little song on her lips Brianna skipped

downstairs and lifted the telephone to set up a date.
Anna agreed immediately. She would be happy to
look at another set of walls, she kidded, and more
importantly, wanted Brianna to see how much more
beautiful her daughter had become in the few days
since she had last seen her.

Next came the hard part. Brianna paused with her
finger on the disconnect button until she had her
breathing under control and had practiced saying
Ryder's name until it came out smoothly and with just
the right amount of friendliness instead of shaky and
too intense. She knew it was going to be very important not to push him in any way.

A bored feminine voice answered her rings.

"The Sun."

Brianna was momentarily attacked by a return of
nervousness and she was glad that she could gather
her courage with a stranger.

"Is Ryder Cantrell there, please?" She was satisfied that her tone was just right. She knew Ryder was
at the paper because Anna had told her he had left
their house a short time before with the expressed
intention of stopping there. The nature of his position
seemed to reflect a certain amount of independence.
He certainly didn't keep regular hours.

"I'm not sure," the voice said. "Who's calling?"

"Brianna St. Clair."

"Just a minute."

Brianna was summarily put on hold and the dead-
ness of the line was broken only by a periodic faint
clicking sound. But at least *The Sun* didn't have that

horrible canned music that made a person want to grind his teeth.

Soon a louder click signaled that the line was being opened again.

"Brianna?" Ryder's husky rendition of her name caused her to break out in goose bumps. She cradled the receiver a little closer to her ear.

"Yes, it's me."

There was a pause. "What can I do for you?"

Love me? Brianna's mind answered. But this time she curbed her impetuous tongue and said instead, "You can say you'll come to dinner at my place tomorrow—or rather your place. Anna and Paul are coming," she rushed on when she thought she detected a little hesitation. "They're going to bring Rebecca."

"Tomorrow?"

"At eight. I'm planning to have the meal ready for about eight-thirty."

"You're cooking?"

Brianna tried to smile. "Don't sound so shocked. I'm a pretty good chef when I want to be. Have you ever tasted a stuffed pork chop?"

"No."

"That's what I'm making."

"Sounds good."

"You'll come?"

"I'll be there."

"Great!"

All at once her mind went blank. What did she say now? She hadn't planned past getting him to agree!

"Well, I guess I'll let you get back to your work." How very original! Lord, she was dazzling him with her dialogue.

"Okay, see you tomorrow. And, Brianna, thanks for the invitation."

"Sure. Bye."

While Ryder hung up his end, Brianna continued to stand with the receiver balanced on her shoulder, her green eyes glowing with anticipation. He was coming! She would see him again soon!

She was going to need a new dress.

The dress Brianna chose was of a clear jewel green that exactly matched the color of her eyes. It was made of a soft, flowy material that wasn't too dressy, yet could be if the occasion arose. And it showed off her femininity in a way that made the most of her really spectacular shape.

As she stood before the mirror twisting to see her reflection from all sides, Brianna had to admit that this evening she had outdone herself. Her hair was looking its best—all thick and golden with just the right amount of curl and body to make it appear as if an aureole of sunshine had come to rest on the exposed silken skin of her shoulders. Her artful touch of makeup complemented a glowing complexion that had little to do with artifice, the touch of blush on her cheeks only partially administered from a tiny glass vial. And her dress—it clung with a soft drape of material over her breasts, exposing just the right degree of swelling womanhood, with thin spaghetti straps on each side. The bodice was nipped in at her small waist by a wide belt of the same material, and the skirt flowed in a glorious crepe fall that revealed a length of shapely leg. Brianna twirled about once again on her delicate silver heels and was satisfied.

She paused only to add a touch of the expensive, flowery perfume she had rewarded herself with after signing her last contract, and then she left her room. But the delicious aroma that floated up from the kitchen to flirt with her senses when she moved into the hallway made her wonder at her surge of vanity. And she smiled dryly to herself as she wondered if Ryder would even remember she was alive between his first step across the threshold and his final push away from the table after repletion.

Ah, but that was the curse of being such a good cook, she teased herself. Men beat a path to your door—but only to taste your chops...pork, that is.

Brianna gave a nervous giggle, then bit her lip to stop the sound. She had to control herself! She was acting like a nine-year-old! And that wouldn't do at all! Not when she was supposed to be a sophisticated vamp. In some disguise, that was true, but it was the direction she had written for herself. Ryder had said he found it hard to leave her alone. Well, she was going to do her best to make it even harder for him. She wasn't going to be obvious, make him regret his confidence to her. But she was damn sure going to take advantage of his stated weakness.

Only things didn't work out quite as Brianna had planned. Ryder was late for dinner for one thing. In

fact she had come to the point where she had given up
on him entirely and was about to start service—Paul,
Anna, and little Rebecca having arrived exactly on
time—when, at last, the doorbell rang.

"That's got to be him," Paul commented. "He's
rarely late if he can help it."

Brianna wrestled with the sudden jangling of her
emotions. In one way she was angry. Had he stayed
away on purpose? Just to show her that he could? Yet
another part of her forgave him anything and hoped
that it was him waiting for admittance.

She moved to the door, her legs curiously unsteady.
It had seemed so long since she had last seen him, and
it was only two days.

Ryder's smile was more than a little rakish as he
stood on the outer narrow porch.

"Am I too late?" he asked.

His eyes moved appreciatively over Brianna's sil-
houetted form, which was all he could see with the
entryway's light coming from behind her.

A fine vibration started in Brianna's stomach and ex-
panded until she was tingling all over. The light from
the interior of the house was shining fully onto him,
and she was instantly struck by the tremendous impact of his brand of potent sexuality. Virility seemed
to be a part of him—like breathing. And it was all she
could do not to throw herself into his arms and press
her lips against his, blending their forms, until he became as intoxicated by her body as she was with his.

"Brianna?"

It took his gruff question to bring her out of her

fantasy. But she still retained a measure of dazed preoccupation as she mumbled a hasty "No, of course not." And motioned for him to come in.

He was dressed in another three-piece suit, the material dark and somewhat formal. His shirt was white, topped by a conservative striped tie. But no one could have worn the look better. His dark hair, with its inclination to curl, was combed into place; his tanned skin showed up even more against the whiteness of the shirt; and he exuded an innate confidence that appealed to something basic in Brianna—appealed strongly, as it had from the very beginning.

As she shut the door behind him, Brianna was extremely conscious of his gaze making a thorough examination of her clothing and body. And the tingling became even more intense. She could feel the heat of the twin blue flames as they moved and then paused, lingering on an area of interest, before moving on again. Her color was a shade pinker than usual as she moved gracefully beside him.

"Paul and Anna are in the living room," she forced herself to say informatively.

"Did you wait for me?"

He was walking so closely to her that she sensed his low husky question was more than just minor curiosity. And that there was more of an emphasis on the word *you*.

"Yes," she returned, then decided to be completely truthful because that seemed to be what he wanted. "But I had almost given up."

He said nothing, however the line of his mouth relaxed, and when Paul lifted himself from his seat on the couch beside Anna to greet his friend, Brianna decided Ryder looked pleased.

"Hey! It's about time you showed up! We were getting tired of waiting." Paul was grinning widely.

"So Brianna tells me." Ryder looked about the room. "Where's Rebecca?"

Anna crossed one slim leg over the other as she remained seated on an overstuffed cushion. "In the bedroom sound asleep. And don't go in and wake her up! Love her though I do, I deserve a little time to myself."

"She was up all last night," Paul added. "She seems to get her days and nights mixed up sometimes."

"Don't we all," Ryder agreed with some degree of mystery.

Paul looked at him curiously. "Where were you?"

Brianna had wanted to ask that very question but had restrained herself. It was something only an old friend could ask with impunity.

Ryder smiled and shook his head. "If I told you *I* was asleep, would you believe me?"

"Yes. But I'd like to know the story behind the story."

Anna reached out to tug on her husband's hand. "Paul! That's Ryder's business!"

Paul ignored his wife. "Does it have something to do with what you were working on last month?"

Ryder's smile disappeared. "How did you know?"

"Just a guess."

The two men continued to look at each other and Brianna gave Anna a puzzled glance. She too was looking at Ryder and there was a high level of concern in her expression.

Finally Anna spoke. "Ryder, you should leave well enough alone. They almost killed you last time!"

Brianna's heart turned cold, or at least it felt that way.

Ryder shrugged. "Not really."

"Almost being run down by a speeding car isn't almost being killed?"

"The one thing probably didn't have anything to do with the other."

"That's not what you said right after it happened!"

"I was overreacting."

Paul's jaw clamped tightly, then he took up where Anna left off. "Whether it was or wasn't, they're still a dangerous group to take on."

Ryder lifted his shoulder again, then angled a glance toward Brianna's pale face. His eyes held hers momentarily, then he smiled again.

"Did you say dinner is ready?"

Brianna had to find her voice. Ryder had almost been run down? He was doing a story on someone that dangerous?

"Ah—yes."

"Then let's eat. I don't know about the rest of you, but I'm starved!"

He looked from one to the other, his lazy smile very much in evidence. Paul and Anna exchanged glances. Brianna could almost hear their minds working—they knew there was no stopping Ryder when he was determined. And he seemed determined to do this...whatever it was.

At that moment Brianna decided that someone was going to tell her what was happening. If Ryder wouldn't, and she didn't know if she should ask, then Anna would. She would force her to if she had to.

However Anna didn't need much forcing. After dinner, when the two women had each quickly dismissed the men's offer of help, almost as if each was equally eager to have the other alone, Anna had barely got into the kitchen before she turned to Brianna and said, "Brianna, do you think you could talk some sense into that man?"

Brianna looked into Anna's expressive face and saw the worry. She didn't need to ask whom they were talking about. "Me?"

Anna made a helpless motion.

"He won't listen to us. Maybe he will to you."

"Again I say, me? The last time we talked about Ryder you warned me away from him."

Anna moved to rest on a kitchen chair. She was frowning. "I know I did, but things have changed."

Brianna took a chair across from her. Had Anna noticed something different in Ryder's behavior?

"Don't you think I should know what you're talking about first? I gather that Ryder is in some kind of danger?"

"He's determined to write a story about some local people who are involved in smuggling aliens into the United States from Mexico."

"Oh!"

"And that's not the worst of it. They stuff them into vans or trucks or whatever—and then rob them and sometimes rape the women after they cross the border."

Brianna's eyes widened. She had heard of those kind of happenings. And Ryder was involved in trying to uncover them?

She thought hard for a moment. "But if *you* know about this, don't the authorities as well?"

"Sure."

"So?"

"It's called evidence. The people here in San Antonio aren't the ones who do the actual smuggling. Someone else does it for them. They're just behind it. The only reason Paul and I know about this is because Ryder told some of it to us after— But he didn't name names. He wanted to protect us."

"Oh, God!"

"Exactly," Anna agreed grimly.

A silence stretched between them.

"And you think I can make him stop?"

"It would be a long shot."

"Then why—"

"Because maybe if you talk to him he'll be more careful."

"He's not careful already?"

Anna shook her head. "He never has been before. It was as if he didn't care."

"You mean about living?" Brianna experienced another cold chill.

Anna's shrug was the same as Ryder had previously used.

As the two of them finished clearing the dishes from the dining room table and washed the pots and utensils that the dishwasher wouldn't hold, Brianna couldn't free herself from the worry that had come to settle on her mind. Gone were all the frivolous plans to make him love her. All she wanted now was for him to place more value on his life. For him to be careful...for him to live! If he didn't want to be with her, she could stand that. It would be hard, but she could stand it. But if he were to die, or to be badly hurt....

Brianna was silent as she and Anna left the kitchen, neither of them having departed from the privacy of their own thoughts for the half hour it took them to finish.

Ryder and Paul were in the living room and little Rebecca was in Paul's arms.

"She woke up," he told his wife, his brown eyes reflecting his pride.

"So I see," Anna responded, the first light of a smile entering her eyes since the round of forced happiness at the table earlier.

Brianna felt Ryder's gaze settle upon her but couldn't meet it yet. If she did, her entire soul would be there for him to read. She slipped quietly into a chair a distance away from him.

A message passed between husband and wife, and Paul instantly rose to his feet, causing the baby to screw up her little face and let forth a tiny mewing sound.

"I think we'd better leave," he stated with an underlying brusqueness that wasn't easy to overlook.

"So soon?" Ryder questioned, his suspicion quickened by Paul's abrupt decision.

"Yeah, I think so. Rebecca needs to be fed and—"

"Anna could feed her here."

Rebecca's tiny sounds increased.

Paul looked down at his daughter and then to Anna for help.

"I'm tired, Ryder." She promptly came to her husband's aid. "I was up with the baby all night last night. So if you don't mind, Brianna...."

Brianna shook her head just as she was supposed to.

Anna smiled. "Thanks for the delicious dinner. I want you to be sure to give me that recipe before you leave."

"Leave?" Ryder repeated.

Anna looked at him. "She isn't going to stay here forever, you know."

Ryder said nothing and Anna glanced back to her husband. "Come on, Paul."

Paul gave a nod to Brianna and followed after his wife.

The room was quiet even though it was still inhabited by two people. But since neither of them spoke, the silence remained.

Brianna was racking her brain for a way to broach

the subject of his story, and Ryder—she didn't know what Ryder was thinking, but he didn't seem very pleased with his thoughts.

Then he gave her an inkling of what he was mulling when he asked, "Are you planning to leave soon?"

For some reason that question startled her. It was so far away from her own thoughts. Earlier it would have encouraged her enormously... but not now.

"Leave?"

He frowned with some impatience. "Leave. Go back to Pittsburgh or wherever."

Brianna's green eyes were darkened. "No, well, not tomorrow at any rate."

"Within the next week or so?"

"I'm not sure."

Ryder subsided into silence.

Brianna watched him. He had removed his jacket after dinner and had unbuttoned his vest. She remembered how it felt to be close to him, and without warning she experienced an overwhelming need to be close to him again.

Without thinking her impulse through, Brianna left the protection of her chair and moved to stand in front of his. Then she dropped onto her knees on the rug that covered the polished wood flooring and laid her head on his thigh above his knee, her arms coming out to wrap around his waist.

At first Ryder seemed astonished by her action, then his hand came out and began to stroke her hair.

Tears came into Brianna's eyes. She didn't want to lose him. Not in any way. A tear rolled from beneath her lashes and fell onto the material of his pants. Soon it was followed by another.

Ryder's hand kept up its stroking movements, until, all at once it stopped, and he sat forward, putting his hands on either side of her jaw, his thumbs beside her ears bringing her face upward. When he saw the evidence of the tears she could do nothing about, he looked deeply into her eyes, where the intensity of color was magnified by the moisture swimming in them.

"Ryder?" she questioned when she saw the change of emotion that stirred in the depths of his. At first he had been surprised, then a shadow had covered the midnight blueness and a kind of suffering began to mark the lines of his face.

He dropped his hands and gently pushed her away.

"It's no good, Brianna," he grated huskily, rising from the chair. She remained on the floor, looking up at him.

"I don't understand," she whispered, bleeding a little on the inside because of his pain.

He raked a hand through his hair and swiveled to look sightlessly about the room.

"Oh, damn it all to hell!"

"What is it?" Brianna struggled to her feet.

He didn't answer her right away. Then he said flatly, "I have to go away for a while."

The knot of dread tightened in her chest.

"Where?"

"I can't tell you."

"Why?"

"I can't tell you that either."

Brianna took a shallow breath. "Does it have something to do with what you and Paul were talking about earlier?"

Ryder's gaze held hers. "Anna told you."

"Yes."

His jaw tightened and he muttered an expletive under his breath.

"She thought that—that I—"

Brianna didn't have time to finish her mutilated sentence as with growing anger Ryder growled, "She thought what? That you could make me not want to go? That if you tried hard enough, even produced a few tears, and told me you were leaving, I'd change my mind?"

Brianna was standing so near all he had to do was reach out to pull her close to him. She could feel the taut emotion that was in possession of his body.

"Well, she was right," he stated fiercely. "I don't want to go anymore. The only thing I can think of right this minute is getting you out of that dress. I want to kiss you and touch you and make love to you until you want me so badly that nothing else in the world matters. I want to be the one to show you what physical pleasure can be. Be the one you think about when you write those hot love scenes in your books. I want to stay here and make love to you over and over again until neither of us has any energy left. Then I'd like to hold you in my arms until we sleep... and wake up with you in the morning." His hands were moving over her back, pressing her against him, making her wholly aware of his burning need.

Yet the next moment she was being pushed away and he was looking at her, his breathing hard, his eyes glittering like pieces of blue jet.

"But I can't do that, Brianna," he grated roughly. "As much as I want to, I can't do it. People are depending on me, and for once in my life I'm not going to let them down!"

Brianna remained motionless, meeting the strength of determination in his steady gaze.

Then she watched with a hollow, growing ache as he stepped away from her and said softly, "Don't bother to see me out. I know the way."

Chapter Nine

Brianna didn't sleep at all that night; she didn't even try. If Ryder had slept during the day, then that meant he was planning on leaving San Antonio that very night. And she didn't know where he was going, if he was alone, what kind of protection he would have, if any, which was the worst kind of misery to her. Because even though she had been so long in making the discovery of her love, that fact didn't take away from its intensity. And whether he loved her or not didn't matter. She loved him.

The hours of darkness were long and her memories of him were clear.

As the first light of day was beginning to chase shadows from the land, Brianna moved restlessly on the couch. The dress she had worn the evening before with such high Machiavellian hope now mocked her. Was it possible for someone, who had long ago thought they were emotionally mature, to grow up even more in such a short period of time?

What she felt for Ryder wasn't part of some strategically planned scheme any longer, one that she could win or lose. When she thought back to her determination to make him care for her, she cringed. She had been such a child! Had so very few minutes passed?

Repeatedly she heard the low, intense echo of his words as he told her what he wanted to do. And the ache inside her grew. She wanted it too! She wanted him with such a fierce inner need that the emotion seemed to have created a life of its own within her.

And, as well, she again heard his harshly spoken denial, his reason for not being able to do as he wanted.

Ryder was an extremely complex personality. She had sensed that from the first. One moment he was relaxed and easygoing, with that lazy smile resting comfortably on his lips, making comments that both irritated and intrigued, and then the next he did something that totally complicated that perception.

He had said that people were depending on him and that for once in his life he was not going to let them down. With what she was privileged to know about him, was that a manifestation that his parents' and his sister's death still had some kind of hold on him? Anna had said he blamed himself—did he still? Was his job at the newspaper, writing columns that tried to right some of the wrongs perpetrated against people, some form of retribution in his view? Was he driven even more than his friends suspected by the ghosts of his past? Was that why he didn't worry about his own well-being?

Anna had said that he held himself aloof, that he distanced himself emotionally from those he helped, that women seemed unable to exert any kind of permanent hold on him, and if they thought otherwise, they were disappointed. And he, himself, had told her he had more in common with antiheroes than heroes. Did he see himself as one?

Brianna groaned. It would be so wrong if he did! He wasn't perfect—no one was! But he wasn't such a horrible person either. He seemed to try to do his best. He had not made love to her when he could have the first time they met. Didn't that show an active conscience? And when it had appeared that he had gone out of his way to hurt her, he had apologized. Then when he found that she was still a virgin, he hadn't ridiculed her as so many men today would. And he hadn't tried to force her into bed when her stupid, inexperienced qualms had given her pause.

Could that be why she loved him?

She didn't know. Could anyone ever say exactly why they loved? They just did.

As a wordsmith, Brianna was admitting a loss of ability. But possibly no one was *supposed* to know the answer. The magic of loving another person transcended mere nouns and pronouns, verbs and adverbs, adjectives and prepositions. It was a gift from the gods, not meant to be dissected by human intelligence. She could write about it, would still write about it. She would live with it, but she couldn't explain it. And she had never felt so humbled.

Yet overriding her continued discoveries about the richness of her newfound love was her fear for Ryder's well-being.

Should she have told him she would wait for him—wait for as long as it took? That she would be here when he returned? But he hadn't asked. He hadn't even kissed her.

The ringing of the telephone cut into her revolving thoughts and she jumped at the sound.

Her heart was pounding as she hurried into the hall to answer it and when Anna's voice responded to her anxious hello, she sagged against the staircase wall.

"Brianna?" Anna asked. "Is that you?"

Brianna tried to control her jumping nerves. Why couldn't it have been Ryder?

"Yes." Her heart was still pounding only now with a sick kind of worry. "Has something happened?"

Anna hesitated before answering. "I was just going to ask you that. Is Ryder still with you?"

"No." It was close to impossible to speak, the pressure in her throat so tight it was nearly closed.

"Then it didn't work."

"No."

Anna gave a long sigh. "Well, it was worth a try." She paused again. "Are you all right?"

A short laugh almost escaped Brianna's lips. "Who? Me? Oh, I'm fine. Just fine."

The tension she had lived with throughout the night caused a rush of tears to come into her eyes, and she reached up to rub the overflow from her cheeks with trembling fingers.

"You're not," Anna decided quickly. "Do you want me to come over?"

"No!"

"Are you sure? You don't sound very good." There was another hesitation, then, "Do you love him that much?"

Brianna did laugh at that, but Anna could easily hear the anxiety behind her laughter.

"You do." There was a dread quality to her words.

Brianna tightened her grip on the receiver. "Yes."

"I didn't know! I thought you were just attracted to him!"

"You warned me."

"I should have kept my mouth shut!"

"It didn't make any difference. I think it was already too late by then."

"He'll be safe, Brianna," Anna tried to reassure her. "It's probably not as bad as I made out. He—he can take care of himself. He has for the past thirty-eight years, so why can't he for the next few days?" When Brianna remained silent, Anna went on, "Trust him, Brianna!"

"But you said he doesn't care about himself!"

"Well, maybe he does now. He's been different with you."

A ray of light came into Brianna's dark world. "How?"

"I think you might have managed to break through some of that wall he's had around himself. But it's been there for years, so it's pretty tough."

Brianna gave another shaky laugh, but this time it was edged with a touch of hope for the future. "Sometimes all it takes is a little crack!"

"And then the wall crumbles!" Anna completed.

"I hope so."

"So do I."

For the moment Brianna felt better. But after she disconnected from Anna's positive reinforcement, the constant companion she had spent the past twelve hours with returned, and she was again plunged into deep depression.

The next two days were the worst Brianna had ever lived through in her life. At no time was Ryder away from her mind. She couldn't work; she couldn't sleep in anything but short, sporadic catches. She merely existed.

The one highlight seemed to be the time when the newspaper was put on the stands. She was like a vulture, waiting. The delivery man barely had time to close the case before she was placing her quarter in the coin slot to snatch her copy. Then she would walk back to the house on King William and turn to the section where Ryder's column appeared. The articles had been prepared in advance, but they were still written by him, retaining the essence of his being. And there was his picture.

The first afternoon Brianna had carefully cut the photo from the newsprint and placed it on her bedside table. It was an excellent likeness—the features rugged and somewhat irregular, yet coming together in a way that was extremely appealing. She even went so far as to run her fingers over the springy dark hair and try to kiss the mouth with its slanted smile. Somehow that helped.

The third day Brianna's body refused to continue the job of functioning without proper rest. Sleep overtook concern while she was sitting in the same chair Ryder had occupied on the night he left. One moment she was aware of the room surrounding her; the next, she was oblivious.

Darkness had settled when she awakened, and she came to awareness with a start. Had she heard something? It sounded like a gunshot! The thought flashed into her mind that she was experiencing some kind of telepathy. She had heard of occurrences like that before. It was a kind of mental communication that transcended the barriers of space. Yet she knew that any small sound tripled its normal size when a person was in the twilight of sleep, and that in all likelihood, the noise she'd heard had been nothing more than a car backfiring. But she couldn't hold back the quick superstitious wish that that was all it was—her overactive imagination, which was usually channeled into her writing, not letting her explain away the happening too easily.

By the fourth morning, Brianna knew she was going to have to get out of the house. Either that or go crazy. She made a quick call to Anna, who had called each previous day, and invited herself to the Daniels's for lunch.

The meal was no joyous occasion. Rebecca, sensing the tensions the adults were experiencing, decided to exercise her lungs, which were already beginning to get quite strong. No longer did she sound like a newborn—she was rapidly developing a very healthy cry. And she seemed not to tire of proving that fact.

Anna apologized profusely, but helping her deal with the cantankerous infant did pass a part of Brianna's afternoon.

When finally the two women had succeeded in quieting the little girl, it was almost time for Paul to check in. He usually did about three, Anna confided, so Brianna waited to hear from him before leaving.

But he had no news of Ryder either. So she went back to the house with her shoulders a little more bent from her downcast mood and her face stiff from trying to pretend that she wasn't as upset as she really was.

As she walked slowly up the pathway and then mounted the short series of steps to the front door, she was wearing a partial smile, because the thought had just occurred to her that she could just see herself and Paul and Anna. All three of them had been trying so hard to convince the others that they were only minimally concerned. If awards were given for acting in real life, each of them had definitely earned one.

She released the latch and moved into the hall, relocking the door behind her. Then she gave a sigh and started to walk toward the kitchen. Coffee had been the mainstay of her diet over the last few days, one more cup would make little difference.

Yet as she moved past the living room doorway something caught her eye. She wasn't sure what it was—whether it was a small movement or what—but she tilted her head to one side and took a step back.

It was then that she saw Ryder. He was lounging,

half sitting, half lying, in one of the comfortable matching chairs, and he was watching her from beneath hooded eyes.

For a moment Brianna stood absolutely still. Was her vision conjuring up his form because she wanted to see him so very much, or was he truly there?

Then he moved. He sat up a little more, and her eyes widened as she saw that his left arm was bandaged just below the elbow.

"Ryder?" she questioned, the disbelief in her voice warring with her desire that he not be an apparition.

"A little the worse for wear..." he confirmed dryly as his blue gaze continued to watch her through narrowed eyelids. Had her entry awakened him?

Brianna stated the obvious. "You're hurt!"

"Not very badly."

Any hurt was too much! She wanted to run to him, but he didn't seem very receptive. So in an agony of indecision she asked another question. "How long have you been here?"

"A couple of hours."

And she had been across town! Why did she have to pick today of all days to go out for all that time?

"How did you get in?" It was hard fighting against the clamoring of her senses.

"I still have a key."

A few seconds of silence passed. Then Ryder said, "Aren't you going to ask me if I got what I went for?"

Brianna nodded.

He smiled. "I did."

"I'm glad." Her answer was scarcely above a whisper. She couldn't stop looking at his arm. To what degree was he injured? She couldn't rely on his "not very badly." "Have you been to a doctor?"

His smile deepened. "Yes. A good one."

"And?"

"Like I said, it's just a graze. I'll hardly know it's there in a few days."

Brianna closed her eyes. So there *was* something to that telepathic incident! She swallowed tightly.

"How did it happen?"

"I was in the wrong place at the wrong time. I'll survive."

Suddenly Brianna experienced an upsurge of blistering anger. How *dare* he take such reckless chances with his life! Not when worry about him had driven her almost half out of her mind!

"But next time you might not!" she snapped, moving further into the room, her green eyes showing sparks of fire.

"That's true," he agreed, a growing light of devilment creeping into the curl of his smile. "Were you worried about me?"

For a time all Brianna could do was to stare at him. Of all things for him to ask! Would she have been concerned about her heart if it had decided to pack up and leave for a few days? Would she have missed her soul?

But as a reaction to his cavalier approach to her possible upset, Brianna found that she couldn't admit to that revealing emotion even if the continued existence of the entire universe was hinging upon her truthfulness. And frustration only increased her irritation.

"No, I didn't miss you," she answered tartly. Then compounded the fabrication by adding, "I was too busy."

Ryder's easy smile of amusement increased. "You don't make a very convincing liar."

Brianna's chin lifted. "Maybe that's because I'm not lying." She searched for something with which to give evidence. "As a matter of fact, I've done everything I need to do here. Enough, so that I don't need to stay any longer."

The room was silent for a moment. Then Ryder, the humor leaving his expression, sat forward and pushed to his feet.

Brianna held herself rigidly still. Oh, God. Why had she said that? She didn't want to leave Texas...or San Antonio...or him! Not now!

"When?"

She knew she couldn't back down and responded tightly, "Saturday. I just have to confirm my reservation."

The tired lines that marked Ryder's face ran deep. "Then in that case I guess I'd better say good-bye to you now." He took the few steps that separated them. "Things are going to be pretty involved for the next few days, so I might not see you again."

It was ending this flatly? He was going to let her go just like that?

"I suppose." Brianna's throat was constricted with

words that wanted to be said, yet remained unvoiced. Bravely she held out her hand.

Ryder gazed at the fingers that were waiting for his. Then he looked up at her. "Don't you think that's a little formal? We've never bothered with customs before."

Brianna kept her hand steady. Maybe, just maybe, she could stand a quick handshake. But if he touched her in any other way.... There was no emotion in her eyes as her gaze held his.

Ryder gave a deep sigh and reached out to enfold her fingers. His skin was warm and vital in comparison to the coolness of hers. He held her hand for a long second before letting it drop away.

"Do you remember when we first met?" he asked.

The unexpectedness of his question made Brianna give an inward start. How could she forget?

"Yes." She found enough courage to answer him calmly.

"You said you'd dedicate your next book to me. Well, don't use my name—just say it's for the villain of the piece and I'll know."

Brianna thought her heart was going to split in two! Why couldn't she tell him? Why couldn't she say the words? But she was determined she was not going to be like the other women who had been in his life. She wasn't going to cling when he didn't want her to.

"All right," she agreed huskily and even managed a small smile. She watched as he started for the door. Then, in a moment of almost unbearable pain, she made one last attempt to bring him back.

"Ryder?" Her voice was high and taut sounding. "Why were you here? Did you need something from me—want me to do something?"

Ryder stopped and turned slowly around. His blue eyes, coming to hers, were weary now as well.

"I think I just got a little confused. I thought there was something here I had left behind. But there wasn't."

Brianna frowned. What did he mean? She had found nothing of his here. Then, as an improbable idea began to form in her brain and take on more credibility as the seconds passed, she whispered awestruck, "Ryder, do you mean me?"

But Ryder was no longer there. And she was left to curse herself for falling into the destructive pit of talking when she should have been listening.

Chapter Ten

Brianna awakened Saturday morning with a grudge against the world. She knew she had only herself to blame for the position she now found herself in, but it hurt too much to admit that. It was much easier to blame Ryder. He had accepted her decision so coolly! Why couldn't he have insisted that she not leave? Why couldn't he have taken her in his arms and used the method he knew so well to convince her to change her plans? Why couldn't he have told her that he loved her? Couldn't he have lied, just a little? No— oh, no! He had other things to take care of. He had an exposé to write! And he had to practice making those Sphinx-like utterances that left a person unsure whether he was standing on his feet or his head!

Damn him! She didn't care! She didn't care at all. It didn't bother her one bit that he had been as good as his word and had not called or come by during the past two days. She didn't mind that from his behavior he wouldn't have even noticed if she had fallen off the edge of the earth and disappeared into a black hole.

Brianna was far from being a saint. And this morning, with an eleven-o'clock flight looming in front of her like an ominous, all-enveloping fog, she was even further from that blessed state.

She hated this house! She hated San Antonio! She hated Texas! Once she set foot on Pennsylvania soil she was never going to let her feet rise from it again. And she was especially not going to write the book she had put all those hours into researching. That idea was as dead as the proverbial doornail. In her mind she gave the characters who were struggling to gain life a beautiful funeral.

Brianna took one last tour of the house to be sure that she had packed everything. She didn't want to leave even the smallest portion of herself here. When she went into the living room, she paused beside the chair Ryder had used and kicked it. The action felt so good that she kicked it again.

It was only the ringing telephone that saved the chair from total annihilation. Brianna hobbled into the hall, her bare toes reddened by their contact with the strong material. Then she saw her reflection in the gilt-edged mirror and couldn't help giving a trembling laugh. If only her fans could see her now! Her hair was tumbled, her pajama blouse was buttoned incorrectly—she had been in no mood to worry about anything last night—and she had just criminally abused an innocent chair. Her laughter bordered on being uncontrollable.

Then she forced herself to calm down. She didn't want to give the impression that she was coming apart at the seams to whoever the caller might be. Who knew? It could possibly be Ryder finally condescending to make contact.

But it wasn't. And the last, valiant, stubborn flower of Brianna's hope withered and died from lack of care.

"Brianna?" Anna asked softly.

Brianna had to swallow a sudden rush of tears. She had never felt so desolate before in her life.

"It's me—Anna."

"I know," Brianna choked.

Anna sighed. "You sound really terrible. I wish you'd reconsider. You're making a horrible mistake!"

"No, I don't think so."

"Well, I do! Ryder was here just a little bit ago. And he looked pretty miserable himself—especially when I got through with him. I told him he was stupid to let the past get in the way of the present."

"You told him that?"

"Yes—and a lot more."

"What did he say?"

There was a little silence. "Well . . . nothing."

Brianna's shoulders slumped and her chin fell. She gave a small, sad laugh. "Matchmaking isn't what it used to be, is it?"

Anna groaned. "That isn't what I was trying to do!"

"I know."

A few more seconds of silence stretched, then Anna said, "At least he's finished with the story—it's going to be in today's paper. And it's not going to be on the feature page. It's headline stuff. He told us a little about it. Do you want to hear?"

Brianna nodded, forgetting that Anna couldn't see.

Anna took her muteness as agreement. "I may have already explained part of this to you, but I'll do it again because it's important to know so that you can understand everything else that follows. A man came to Ryder a month or so ago, an informant. He told him about two men who live here in the city and have ties to—I think the term he used was 'coyotes.' Anyway, they're the people who smuggle aliens into the country and then do all kinds of horrible things to them before they let them go. And sometimes they don't just let them go—sometimes people die. Well"— she took a breath—"this man had information and Ryder started to check it out. That was when he had the accident. We think that it was these people's way of trying to discourage him. But you know Ryder. Discourage him? It made him mad! And he's been working on the story ever since. Kind of on the quiet and on the side. Paul and I certainly didn't know about it until that night at your house."

Brianna's thoughts instantly went to the time Ryder was waiting to meet a man at the institute. Had that been to get more information?

Anna continued. "When he had enough evidence to convince him what he had been told was true, he went to the authorities, thank God. But they had to have more evidence—which meant catching the men in the act. That was what his trip was about. They let Ryder come along—let him, mind you—with the promise that he could break the exclusive story. And what made it all the more interesting was that one of the men involved is the son of a woman high up in local politics. *And* there are implications that she knew what was going on."

"My Lord."

"Exactly."

"Have arrests been made?" Brianna was suddenly concerned for Ryder's continued safety.

"The men who did the actual smuggling were arrested before Ryder came back. Then when they decided to cooperate, warrants were made up for the two here. They're in custody now as well."

"Will they stay that way?" Brianna's active imagination jumped to a replay of every television crime show she had ever seen.

"I should think so. Ryder says they're in pretty tight."

A trembling breath left Brianna's lips.

Anna heard and prompted, "Why don't you cancel your flight...stay here for a few more days. What could it hurt?"

Me, Brianna thought. *A lot!* It would be three more days for Ryder to show that he didn't care. And she didn't think she could stand that. These past two had been more than enough!

"My family's expecting me."

"You could call them."

"No."

"I can't say anything to make you change your mind, can I?"

Again Brianna silently shook her head. And again Anna knew what she was doing. Sadly she acquiesced to Brianna's wishes.

"You will keep in touch, won't you?" she begged. "When I first met you I was proud to know you because of who you are. But almost immediately, I forgot you're so well known and started to like you for you."

Tears once more came into Brianna's eyes. "Thank you, Anna. That means a lot to me."

"Paul wanted me to tell you he sends his love."

"Tell him I send mine back. And kiss little Rebecca for me. I— Maybe someday you can come visit me in Pennsylvania. I'd like that."

"We'll sure try. I'll send you pictures."

Brianna murmured an agreement then hung up the telephone before she made a complete idiot out of herself. She had to blink several times in order to clear her vision enough to see that she had barely an hour left before she had to begin her drive to the airport.

Brianna observed the bustling activity at the airport with pain-dulled eyes. All of her anger had evaporated in the seconds following Anna's call. No longer did she blame Ryder. But neither could she blame herself. That she had fallen in love was no one's fault. It had just happened. It was a part of life. Just as was the hurt she was now experiencing. People couldn't be made to return emotions on order. Ryder had been hurt badly long before she had happened into his life—and if he had experienced any stirring of feeling for her at all she supposed she should be happy with that. At least it was something. She might have been like the other women who had touched his life—with everything totally on her side.

Yet she couldn't help the vulnerable ache that resulted from the bleeding open sore. She had read about hearts being pierced, but she had never thought to experience it. And that was exactly how it felt. Cupid's arrow was steel tipped. It left a jagged wound.

Brianna drew a shaking breath. She had come to Texas with such high hopes, and she was leaving with nothing left to hope for. Would she ever heal?

The waiting area was slowly filling up. Families, businessmen—people either going to Pittsburgh to visit or returning from a vacation, with more than one sporting a Western hat and boots—they were to be Brianna's companions on the flight. A woman came to take the seat next to her, but Brianna looked away from her friendly smile. She didn't feel like talking to anyone. She would have to pretend to be happy or at least pleasant, and she felt neither. If only Ryder had come to love her!

Brianna rose to her feet as if she had been a jack-in-the-box and someone had released her spring. No! She wouldn't dwell on that. She couldn't! She would have to do something, find something. She couldn't make the hours-long flight with her mind concentrating on each passing mile that was taking her farther away from the only man she loved.

She checked her watch and saw that there was just enough time to make a quick stop in the airport's gift shop. Surely there would be a book or a magazine that she could purchase to keep her mind occupied. Brianna hurried out of the waiting area.

The gift shop had a little of everything from pornographic "literature," wrapped discreetly in noncommittal paper with only lurid titles showing what was within, to children's story books. Brianna settled for something in between.

Her gaze was immediately drawn to a line of her own books—her second, third, and finally her last, *Wild Desert Flower*. Brianna quickly turned her face away. Was it always going to hurt when she saw the cover of that book? Would it always remind her of Ryder and the first time they had met? She took a few steps away. There were books by Kathleen Woodiwiss, Johanna Lindsey, Laurie McBain. She would choose one of them. She had had little time to read fiction lately. And she knew they were all good writers. She would stand a better chance of involving herself in one of their stories than with some of the other lesser-known authors whose books she scanned. The only problem was they wrote romances. And she wasn't sure if it would be wise for her to read of someone else's problems and eventual happiness. Not when she was so agonizingly aware that reality didn't always reward a person with a happy ending.

Brianna shut her eyes, Kathleen Woodiwiss's latest best seller clutched tightly in her hand. She had her back to the main part of the shop and her face was lowered. So she had no idea of a man's approach until his low husky voice penetrated her thoughts with a request.

"Hey, lady, would you mind giving me your autograph?"

Brianna started. Not so much at his question—how someone would know her identity—but at the familiar quality of his voice. Ryder! It was Ryder!

Her spirit broke the restraints of bondage and instantly began to sing. But before it had warbled more than two notes, Brianna harshly strangled any further signs of joy. He might just have come to say good-bye again, to see her off. She couldn't even begin to hope it would be anything different. Hope was one emotion she had nothing left to show.

Collecting herself, she raised her head as she slowly turned around. She had to brace herself all over again when she looked into Ryder's face. It had the same dear rugged lines, the nose that was a bit too large, the same dark blue eyes ringed with short black lashes, the same lazy smile....

Brianna struggled to keep her reply calm. "Hello, Ryder. What brings you here?"

At her seeming coolness Ryder's expression lost some of its jauntiness, his eyes some of their teasing.

"I could say that I came here to meet a man—but that wouldn't be true."

Brianna swallowed tightly. What was the truth? "Did you come to see me?" she asked, braving whatever would come.

Ryder nodded, his now serious gaze holding hers.

"Why?" the word was a misery for Brianna to say because hope was busy resurrecting itself from the morass of unanswered longing, and the resulting conflict with intellect was causing a gigantic war to rage within her.

"Because I had to."

His simple answer effectively disabled the warrior, intellect, leaving hope the victor. Brianna's heart began to thud more rapidly.

"Why?" Once before she had made the mistake of talking when she should have been listening. This time she was not going to let that happen again!

Ryder didn't flinch at her directness. "Because I've found that I don't want to live without you."

A series of jingling bells sounded in Brianna's ears that soon turned into the announcement system telling all passengers of her flight that they could now board. Brianna noted the request and then ignored it.

"Why?" she persisted.

"I love you."

"Are you sure?"

"I'm sure."

"I don't believe you."

"Then go get on the jet."

"No."

"Why?"

"Because you might be telling the truth."

"And you'd care?"

"Of course I'd care!"

"Why?"

"Because I love you too, you fool! I have for the longest time!"

Brianna didn't care that her voice had risen or that the rest of the patrons of the gift shop were looking at her. She was suddenly coming alive to all the wonders of the world—and the man before her was the one letting it all happen!

Ryder's slanted smile appeared and broadened as what she had said was digested. Then he said, "That has got to be the most unusual declaration of love I've ever heard of."

"Do you mind?" Brianna inquired, a smile dawning on her soft mouth. She took a step closer. She wasn't about to let him get away from her again. She would tackle him if she had to—if he suddenly decided to change his mind and try to get away.

The thought seemed not to have entered Ryder's head. He reached out to pull her against him, unconsciously providing a live reenactment of some of the romantic covers in the background.

"Are you kidding?" he murmured, before bending to fasten his lips to hers.

The kiss started out in a light, teasing frame—a continuation of their last words—but it rapidly changed into a burning exchange that threatened to topple the propriety of San Antonio's morals. It took the pointed clearing of a salesclerk's throat to bring them back to awareness of just where they were.

"I'm going to have to charge you for that book," she stated gruffly.

Brianna unwound her arms from their position about Ryder's neck and looked at the gray-haired woman a little blankly.

"What book?" Ryder asked the question she was trying to form.

"The one that got crushed when the lady dropped it."

Ryder and Brianna shifted a degree so that they could look to where the salesclerk was pointing. Sure enough, on the floor, was the book Brianna had been holding. Only Brianna knew that the cover and pages had not gained the creases when she dropped it; it had suffered the damage earlier when she had been grasping it so tightly after Ryder surprised her.

"I'll gladly pay," she volunteered.

The woman had other things on her mind as well. "And you're going to have to stop all that—that kissing! You can't do it in here. Go to one of the boarding gates—it will fit in fine there."

Brianna stared at the woman in amu ement. At first, when she had demanded payment and sputtered the word *kissing*, she had thought her to be a sanctimonious prig. But by the twinkle that had later entered her faded blue eyes, she was fast changing her mind.

"Better still," the woman urged Ryder. "Take her home. I heard her say she loves you."

Ryder gave a shout of amused laughter. "I agree with you completely." His hands tightened their grip on Brianna's waist. "What do you say? Do you want to come home with me?"

Brianna's green eyes were sparkling with mounting happiness. "More than anything else in the world."

"Then let's go."

The two of them started to walk away, but the woman once again halted their action.

"The book?" she reminded.

"Oh!" Brianna bent to retrieve the paperback and Ryder started to search his inner jacket pocket.

But before he could withdraw the money, the woman surprised them by saying, "Oh, go on. Keep it as a souvenir. It's not every day the boredom of this place gets broken by such...ah...enthusiasm."

Brianna's face took on a pink hue. Had they been that uninhibited?

Ryder bent to kiss the older woman's cheek.

"Thanks," he said softly.

The woman blushed and waved them away.

A short hour later Brianna was lying in Ryder's bed, the silkiness of her skin pressed closely against the bronze smoothness of his. Each of them was breathing hard.

She raised her head from where it was lying on his chest, her long blond hair falling about her shoulders like a tangled golden waterfall.

"I had no idea it could be like that," she whispered, thousands of tiny stars still lighting the depths of her emerald gaze.

"Neither did I," he admitted as well, the huskiness of arousal still shading his words.

"You didn't?" Brianna questioned.

Ryder smiled his slow smile, a look of such satisfaction and love on his face that Brianna's heart twisted. "Nope."

"But you've had other women...surely...."

"You're the first one I've loved."

Brianna smoothed her palm over his cheek and he caught it and kissed it.

"Loving makes that much difference?"

Ryder released her hand and pulled her head back against his chest. His fingers were threaded in her hair as he pressed her close. "Yes."

Brianna shut her eyes. He did love her! He really did! She had believed him and yet.... But now she did totally, and she would never doubt him again.

She turned her cheek until she could kiss the hair-roughened skin that covered hard muscle. Ryder let her work her way upward until he could meet her lips with his. The kiss they shared was long.

They broke apart only after mutual consent, and Brianna burrowed her head back against his shoulder beside his neck. Her breasts tingled where they touched him and there was a warm glow centered deep in her body from use and completion.

It was hard to believe that all of this had happened. This morning she wouldn't have believed it. She had been nothing but a hulk of human misery—leaving, but hating it. Not admitting the truth because it hurt too much to think about. Going through the motions of going home. But now she *was* home—in the truest sense of the word. Wherever Ryder was, that was her home now.

Yet even in the beautiful mists of her newfound joy, there was the knowledge that a dangling thread still needed to be tied. And that until it was, it would forever remain just outside of reach—a hindrance to total communication and sharing. Brianna took a deep breath, her closeness to Ryder giving her courage.

"Ryder." She stayed where she was; she didn't look at him. "Would you tell me something?"

"What?" She heard the rumble in his chest.

"Would you tell me about your wife."

When she felt his abrupt stiffening, Brianna experienced a sick, sinking sensation. She shouldn't have asked him now—not so soon. It had been a stupid thing to do! But she couldn't take the request back! Her fingers tightened against his shoulder.

"What do you want to know?" he asked at last.

"Just... about her. Is she still alive?"

"I suppose."

"Don't you know?"

"I make it a habit not to think of her."

"Is that good? I mean..." Brianna rushed on, feeling his tension heighten even more. "I know it's probably not any of my business, but sometimes when you talk about things that are bothering you, they go away."

Ryder eased her away from him and then sat up, his arms coming to hook over his bent knees. "She doesn't bother me," he denied flatly.

Brianna sat forward as well, one hand behind her back supporting a portion of her weight. "Then why are you pulling away from me?" Her soul quivered in the question.

Ryder heard the hurt plea and looked back at her, startled. "I pulled away?"

"The second I mentioned her."

His blue gaze darkened. "I didn't know that I had."

Brianna tried to give a small smile and measured the distance between them with her eyes. "Look at us."

Ryder immediately closed the gap, his arms coming out to lay her back along the sheet's cool smoothness. Her body was then enfolded with his, his warmth comforting her, the strength of his muscles straining her to him.

"God, Brianna, I didn't mean to do that! I just—"

Brianna tried to soothe him by running her fingers along the crisp hair that grew at his temple. "Shhh. It's all right."

They were silent for a moment, each caught up in their own thoughts even though their bodies were together.

Then Ryder expelled a deep breath and admitted, "Maybe you're right. Maybe I've been going about things the wrong way. Lord knows I've been miserable enough!"

His admission allowed Brianna to ask the question that frightened her most. "Do you still love her?"

Ryder's hand left her lower back and fastened onto her chin, bringing her head upward to meet his gaze.

"Can a person love a black widow spider? No, I don't love her."

Brianna trembled inwardly from relief. "Then why—"

"Have you ever thought you wanted something so badly that you'd die if you didn't get it, and then when you got it you found out that you didn't really want it—that it wasn't what you thought it would be? Well, that's the way it was with Susan and me. We met our first year at the university. She was everything a young man could dream about—beautiful, popular. She was a cheerleader, one of the campus queens, the whole works. And I wanted her. So did every other male there. But for some reason, I was the one she picked out."

Brianna experienced a dark surge of jealousy. She had wanted him to confide. But she wasn't sure if she wanted to go on listening.

"We were married the year we graduated. For the first few months everything was fine. Oh, I noticed a few of the shallow, self-centered things she did, but I tried to ignore them. After a while though, it got harder and harder. And pretty soon she began to be bored with having only me to adore her. Then when I couldn't continue to do that"—he shrugged lightly—"things went from bad to worse. We limped along for a year or two before we separated, and finally, after a time, we divorced. I haven't heard from her since."

"But you still haven't got over her."

Brianna hadn't wanted to say those words—they were like tearing out some of her vital organs—but she had to.

"If you mean that I'm still reacting to the bad experience, well, I'm beginning to see that I was. I thought I had put it all behind me. But I guess, deep down, I was comparing every woman I met to her...and not wanting to make that kind of mistake all over again."

Brianna's heart rate quickened. "What about me?"

Ryder bent his head and gave her lips a quick kiss. "You were different." A smile slanted.

"How?" She caught her breath.

"You just kind of crept in. One minute I didn't know you were anywhere near, and the next, I couldn't get you out of my mind!"

Brianna let the air release. "And were you angry about that?"

"Very. But it didn't do me much good. I did try to stay away."

"You told me that once."

"Yes, and look what happened afterward. Do you realize I've made a spectacle of myself all over town with you? Yet sometimes when you were close to me it was all I could do just to limit myself to a kiss!"

Brianna's spirit was starting to soar again. "What else did you want to do?" she asked innocently, but with warm knowledge in her eyes.

Ryder's hand lowered from its supporting position under her chin and ran down along her neck to the sensitive skin of her upper chest until it gained its target. His fingers spread out over one exposed breast and began to caress it. "I wanted to touch you here, kiss you here...." His hand smoothed lower over her nipped in waist and curving hip. "I wanted to touch you here...." His hand continued its lowering path. "And here...."

Brianna gave a pleasurable gasp as his fingers caressed her boldly. She met the burning look in his eyes.

"I wanted all of you, Brianna," he husked. "I want all of you...for the rest of my life!"

A growing fire was making Brianna's mind almost insensible to all but one thought. She moved to show her enjoyment. That was all the encouragement Ryder needed. His mouth fastened hungrily onto hers. Then when his lips broke away to follow a trail already blazed, Brianna whispered "Yes" softly, almost as if she were sealing a vow.

In the months since Brianna had left Pennsylvania, she found that she had quite forgotten what a northern winter could be like. How the cold wind could blow across the Allegheny and the Monongahela rivers to send chills down an unprotected neck, how it felt to be still having snow storms in late March. San Antonio certainly wasn't experiencing such a thing.

When she and Ryder had left the warm, southern city they laughed about wearing summer things and carrying a coat. But their coats had proved welcome immediately upon landing in Pittsburgh, the area experiencing an ice storm alert.

All day the gods of the north waged a frigid war. And that night, as they prepared for bed in the room allotted to them by her parents, Ryder complained, "Cripes! How do you people stand living in such a place?"

"We're used to it," Brianna responded, reaching in front of him to put her toothbrush back into its case.

Ryder shivered then switched off his electric razor. "I don't think I was meant to leave the South."

"You'd get used to it too."

"You're missing my point—I don't *want* to get used to it!"

Brianna smiled a secret little smile and reached out to put her palms on either side of the bare flesh of his waist. "Maybe if you'd consent to wearing my father's pajamas...."

"Like you're wearing your mother's...whatever-it-is?"

Brianna looked down at the voluminous, but toasty-warm, pink flannel nightgown. Her teasing smile increased. "Don't you think it flatters me?"

Ryder raised an eyebrow. "Just be glad I love you, lady. That's all I have to say!"

Brianna held out the edges of the gown as if it were a ball gown. "*I* think I look ravishing!"

"*You* do. The gown doesn't."

"It keeps me warm."

"*I* keep you warm."

Brianna pretended to pout. "And don't I keep you warm too?"

Ryder's lazy smile appeared. "Sure...in bed."

"Are you cold?"

"Is that a proposition?"

She shrugged, her green eyes alive with love and mischief.

"Because if it is, I'll take you up on it," he quickly agreed.

Brianna gave a strangled gurgle of laughter when Ryder swooped and captured her in his arms. Then he walked to the bed where, instead of lying her on the downturned layers of multicolored quilts, he stood her on her feet.

"First, we get rid of this," he determined, touching the hated thick cotton nightdress. He drew it over her head. "And second, we do this...." His lips lowered to hers in a kiss of such sweet, sensual persuasion that Brianna instantly melted against him, her body fitting into his as if they had always been a part of each other. With infinite gentleness Ryder lifted her into his bed and then came down beside her.

The wind was howling around the eaves of the old house as later Brianna lay curled close to Ryder, the weight of the quilts seeming to make a warm cocoon of their shelter.

"Have I told you lately how much I love you?" Brianna whispered.

"Not in the last minute," her husband returned promptly. "Have I forgotten to tell you how much I love you?"

Brianna burrowed closer. "Not in the last half minute."

Ryder hugged her against him. Those words were fast becoming a ritual between them. One that couldn't be repeated too often.

"My parents like you," Brianna commented contentedly.

"I like them too."

"And my sister is crazy about your accent. She once told me she wanted the man I eventually made her brother-in-law to talk like you do."

Ryder slanted a smile. "I'm glad she's pleased."

Brianna raised her head to look at him closely, resting it on a crooked elbow. "Didn't you lay it on a bit thick though when she complimented you on your boots?"

"It's all part of the game."

"What game?"

"The game that keeps you close to me."

"I didn't know we were playing a game."

Ryder's blue eyes smiled. "We were involved in one from the first second that we saw each other. I thought you were one of the prettiest women I'd ever seen in my life."

"You did?" They hadn't talked very much about the beginning of their relationship. There hadn't been time—they were too involved in creating memories of today. This was the first instance Ryder had broached it. And it pleased her that he was doing so.

"Sure. What did you think about me?"

Brianna began to giggle. "My very first thought?"

"Yes."

"I don't think I should tell you."

Ryder's lazy smile increased. "Why?"

"Because you'll get conceited.

"No, I won't."

Brianna paused for just a second, timing her confession for ultimate impact. "I wanted to get you into bed!"

Ryder gave an immediate shout of laughter that she had to shush him into controlling. "Hush, you'll wake everyone!" she chided although she was laughing softly with him.

"We probably already woke them."

"Ryder!"

"Well, it's the truth."

"Oh, Lord."

"Hey, we're married, remember?"

"I'll never forget! But my parents...."

"Are married too. They know everything that's going on in here."

"That's even worse!"

Ryder was looking at her with amused wonder. "I can't believe it! You're a prude!"

"No, I'm not!"

"Yes, you are! You write all those sexy scenes, you enjoy everything we've done over the past four months to the absolute limit, and now I find out that you're nothing but a wrinkly faced, dried-up old prude!"

Brianna let out a little screech and moved onto her knees so that she could hit at him with her pillow. "Take that back, Ryder Cantrell! Take that back or I'll..."

Ryder was laughing uninhibitedly. "Wrinkly faced old prude!"

"Oh! Oh!"

Suddenly Ryder lunged at the pillow and in the process pushed Brianna over backward, his body quickly following to press his advantage. Dancing blue eyes met incensed green, then slowly the flash of anger left Brianna's gaze.

"You're a mean man, Mr. Cantrell."

"I warned you I was the villain."

"And you are! I'm modeling Raoul Sanchez de Zavala exactly after you."

"Is he going to get the girl?"

"No, he can't. The hero is."

"The one who dies at the siege of the Alamo?"

"You looked at my outline!" she accused.

"I just peeked."

"I wanted that to be a surprise!"

"That the villain gets the girl?"

"No, that the villain wasn't really a villain, he only thought he was."

"Like me?"

"Like you."

Ryder smiled and smoothed her golden hair. "Do you know something?"

"What?"

"I love my wrinkly faced old prude."

Brianna inhaled a fast gulp of air, ready to stage another protest, but Ryder stopped her by covering her mouth with his.

And as soon as some of the heated need of his body transmitted itself to the answering passion of hers, Brianna forgot about her parents—what they might hear, what they might know.

She was Ryder's woman now and that was all that truly mattered.

Harlequin reaches
into the hearts and minds
of women across America
to bring you

Harlequin American Romance ™.

YOURS FREE!

Enter a uniquely exciting new world with

Harlequin American Romance™·

Harlequin American Romances are the first romances to explore today's love relationships. These compelling novels reach into the hearts and minds of women across America... probing the most intimate moments of romance, love and desire.

You'll follow romantic heroines and irresistible men as they boldly face confusing choices. Career first, love later? Love without marriage? Long-distance relationships? All the experiences that make love real are captured in the tender, loving pages of **Harlequin American Romances**.

What makes American women so different when it comes to love? Find out with **Harlequin American Romance!**

Send for your introductory FREE book now!

Get this book FREE!

Harlequin American Romance

Twice in a Lifetime
REBECCA FLANDERS

Mail to:

Harlequin Reader Service

In the U.S.	In Canada
2504 West Southern Avenue	649 Ontario Street
Tempe, AZ 85262	Stratford, Ontario N5A 6W2

YES! I want to be one of the first to discover **Harlequin American Romance.** Send me FREE and without obligation *Twice in a Lifetime.* If you do not hear from me after I have examined my FREE book, please send me the 4 new **Harlequin American Romances** each month as soon as they come off the presses. I understand that I will be billed only $2.25 for each book (total $9.00). There are no shipping or handling charges. There is no minimum number of books that I have to purchase. In fact, I may cancel this arrangement at any time. *Twice in a Lifetime* is mine to keep as a FREE gift, even if I do not buy any additional books.

Name _____ (please print)

Address _____ Apt. no. _____

City _____ State/Prov. _____ Zip/Postal Code _____

Signature (If under 18, parent or guardian must sign.)